I0531628

# Storylandia

## The Wapshott Journal of Fiction

Issue 8

The Wapshott Press

Storylandia, Issue 8, The Wapshott Journal of Fiction, ISSN 1947-5349, ISBN 978-0-9848325-6-9, is published at intervals by the Wapshott Press, PO Box 31513, Los Angeles, California, 90031-0513, telephone 323-201-7147. All correspondence can be sent The Wapshott Press, PO Box 31513, LA CA 90031-0513. Visit our website at www.WapshottPress.com This work is copyright © 2013 by Storylandia. The Wapshott Journal of Fiction, Los Angeles, California. "Dr. Hackenbush Gets Some Culture" is copyright © 2013 Ginger Mayerson is reprinted here with the copyright owner's permission. Copyrights for the cover artwork is held by the artist and is reprinted here with the copyright owner's permission.

Storylandia is always seeking quality original short stories, novelettes, and novellas. Please have a look at our submission guidelines at www.Storylandia.WapshottPress.com or email the editor at editor@wapshottpress.com

Many thanks to Kathleen Warner and Nancy Lilly for the proofreads and editoral support.

Cover: Detail from "La América Tropical", by David Alfaro Siqueiros. http://olvera-street.com/html/siqueiros_mural.html

# Storylandia

## The Wapshott Journal of Fiction

Founded in 2009

Issue 8, Winter 2013

Edited by Ginger Mayerson

## Table of Contents

Ginger Mayerson

# Dr Hackenbush Gets Some Culture

1989

Pamela Tucker was a woman sure of many things. She was sure she was a good painter. She was sure she'd gotten a good foundation in art at East Los Angeles Graphics. She was sure she wanted ELAG, as they called it for short, to succeed, and to that end, she was sure she and eleven other up-and-coming LA artists had done the right thing in copying a rich man's David Alfaro Siqueiros painting as a fund-raiser for ELAG.

She was also sure it was a pretty stupid way to raise money to keep ELAG going. She didn't know who thought it up, but it must have been a pretty twisted mind to have twelve painters set up in the drawing room and copy the Siqueiros so the copies could be auctioned off at this party. It had been cruel. Mr. Vogler, the owner of the Siqueiros, had a buffet lunch set out every day they were there copying, but either from rage or sorrow, none of the copyists ate much of it.

But Pam figured it was all for ELAG, and the new director, a large lady from the east coast, Manuela Something y Something, had new energy, drive and whatever the ELAG board thought it would take to get the school, workshops, and galleries back on their feet. For the past forty years students had received free art instruction from ELAG. It had sparked a few great artists, or as great as Los Angeles allowed any of its artists to be, but it also trained countless teens to be organized, thorough and thoughtful in their work. Some worked in graphics, animation, or the movie industry as artists, but most held down workaday-type jobs, raised their families and let their love of art warm the cold, cold world around them.

It was, Pam had heard, only in the past few years that infighting between the board and a string of poorly chosen local directors had nearly brought ELAG to its knees. Hence the board had brought in new blood and new thinking and, hopefully, a future.

Although she hadn't been there in years (ELAG was quite a ways east of her studio), Pam still loved the place. Someday, she wanted to take her children there for art lessons, if she had any children, and if she didn't she planned to volunteer to teach there. If they'd have her; she'd heard it was Chicanos only these days. Nevertheless, Pam still had deep and profound feelings for the place that taught her how to ruin her clothes with linseed oil and pour her heart out on a variety of media.

So Pam was very sure she'd done the right thing participating in this fundraiser. She was also very sure that the Siqueiros over the fireplace, flanked by six copies on either side, was not the one she'd copied from two weeks ago. She looked at the fingers of her right hand, and then peered into the softly lit garden for inspiration.

"Why am I here? What am I doing here? What have I done to deserve this? Why must I suffer?"

Mabel Hackenbush, vocalist, front-woman and baritone ukulele player extraordinaire for *Dr. Hackenbush and her Orchestra*, leaned over the man in a baggy tuxedo curled into fetal position on the garden bench. She didn't lean too far because her black horn-rim glasses slid down her nose and her form-fitting evening gown gave new meaning to the words 'plunging neckline'; this neckline was deep like the Mariana Trench is deep. "What was that, Arlo?" she snapped. "Speak up, pal, I can't hear a word you're sayin' down there."

Arlo Mega uncurled and leapt to his feet and shook his fist at the oak tree, and presumably the heavens, above them. "I said, why must I suffer?!" He yelled this, so not only Hackenbush but the party guests nearby heard it as well.

"Because you're a great artist, but a fucking disaster in social situations." Hackenbush smiled pleasantly and waved at the people staring at them as she said this. "And if you won't drop this martyred artist pose I will leave you here all by yourself to defend yourself from these art patrons, posers, socialites, and other such weirdoes."

Arlo got a hurt look on his face. "You wouldn't do that to me. I asked you to help me through this ordeal."

"Then straighten up and fly right, Mr. Mega," Hackenbush sighed, adjusting her black horn-rim glasses. "Or at least do your half of the schmoozing. I didn't give up one of my precious nights off to listen to you whine." She pulled his jacket shoulders back into some semblance of order; there was nothing to be done with his hair, which stuck up in coarse black tufts even on good days. "Remember, it's all for a good cause. You like East LA Graphics as much as anyone who studied there."

"This is a stupid way to raise money," Arlo grumbled, pulling his cuffs straight.

"I heard they fed you pretty good lunches," she said, lighting an unfiltered Pall Mall and picking a shred of tobacco off her tongue.

"Food! Who can think of food when you're standing in a room with other artists copying a Siqueiros easel painting, one I'd never heard of, and wouldn't have heard of if this sick obsession white people are having with Frida Kahlo wasn't driving the prices of every dead

Mexican painter through the ceiling. Thanks," he said, accepting a Pall Mall and a light. "Don't get me wrong, Hackenbush, I have nothing against Siqueiros and Kahlo," he continued. "I think it's high time they and that whole scene, except Rivera, got more recognition. It's just having twelve 'up-and-coming' LA painters copy the damn thing so Mr. Lawrence Vogler can show off his Siqueiros that he probably got for a goddam song in the sixties, and then auction off the copies and the money goes to ELAG." Arlo favored her with one of his best sneers. "What a joke. If they really cared, they'd just auction off some of the work in my studio and give me a cut. I'd settle for half."

"You're missing the point so much, I'm not even going to try to explain it to you. Oh, and they don't care, they've never cared, and they're never ever gonna care. So, pull yourself together, Arlo. and face it." Hackenbush was laughing so bitterly, she had a hard time getting that out. "But, honey, I can see why you're insulted," she said, pulling her own self together. "It is kind of an insult that you have to copy the work of someone who's too dead to appreciate it in order to help some artists who are too poor to pay for their own art supplies." She took him by the shoulders and looked deeply into his eyes. "But, Arlo, whoever told you life was fair?" she asked, a touch too dramatically. "Or fun? Or profitable? Or–"

"Nobody, baby, but I wish someone could tell me why a jerk like Vogler gets all this." Arlo waved in a general way at the garden around the mansion nestled in the best part of San Marino. "And you and I pay taxes on our unemployment–"

"When we can get it," she put in.

"–and tip twenty-three percent to cover the fucking waitress tax," he concluded.

"Because we was born just in time to get fucked–"

"–and not even kissed–" he added.

"–by the Reagan Revolution," she finished,

briskly. "Sorry, Arlo, if we're going to fight a class war tonight, we better go home and change out of our good clothes. I, for one, have eaten too much of Vogler's food and drunk too much of his booze to be in the mood to tear down the dominant social group right now." She listened to Arlo's low growl, which meant his mood was improving. "What have you got against Diego Rivera?"

"Nothing," he said. "He's an icon and gets enough press. I like Siqureos, too, murals and easel paintings. I just think this painting has become valuable to Vogler because the price shot up, not because it speaks to his soul or whatever."

"Maybe it speaks to his wallet. Does it speak to your soul?" she asked.

Arlo hesitated. "No. It's not a strong piece compared to Siqueiros' other work," he said. "But right now you can't judge a famous dead Mexican artist by what his work is worth, only what it costs."

"Welcome to the late 20th century, Arlo," Hackenbush murmured under her neutral smile. Truth be told, she wasn't enjoying her evening much either. There were too many annoying people at this party. For one thing, her ex-fiancé and ex-guitar player, Eddy Lee, was there with his trio as the entertainment. Yes, they were playing some very tasteful and occasionally tasty low-key jazz, but it annoyed her to see him working when she was not. Even though he was on the bandstand, she was the one who felt like the show.

"Well, we're not the only ones suffering tonight," Arlo said, failing to notice Hackenbush was a million miles away just then.

Another stressor for Hackenbush was Renee Soleil, vocalist, hellcat, and Eddy Lee's ex-girlfriend prior to Hackenbush. Being in the same species as La Soleil was hard on Hackenbush; add in being dumped by Eddy Lee in common with her was just injury onto insult.

"I mean, all the painters are here," Arlo went on, feeling he had her full attention because she wasn't interrupting. "They all brought dates or spouses, so that's times two. Except for the ones who are twisted enough to like this kind of thing."

Vogler's son, Emil, was pissing Hackenbush off as well. He and Janet Tran, who was practically his fiancée, were strutting around like they not only owned the place, but owned everyone in it.

"It's all window dressing, Hackenbush," Arlo said darkly. "Have a party, sprinkle in a few wacky but housebroken artists for color, not because you understand, God forbid appreciate, their work, but just because it's the vogue right now."

However, Hackenbush, like anyone with a ear for gossip, knew that bitch Janet Tran was sleeping with Eddy Lee for fun, and Emil Vogler for status.

"Take Linda Lim," Arlo said, perking up a little. "One of the best sculptors alive today. Vogler wouldn't understand her work if it was surgically implanted in him."

It was Janet Tran who'd organized this fundraiser. She was some kind of photographer, scene-ster, aspiring art maven, talent-less wench who took pictures to get attention, not because she had any soul or vision.

"Shorty Smith is here," Arlo said. "I'd bet money Vogler has never seen you two dance in his life."

This got Hackenbush's attention. She'd been dancing with Shorty even before she met Eddy Lee. It was comforting to see Shorty in the swanky crowd milling around the patio, nattily dressed and adorable as ever, standing next to his current boyfriend, the not-so-swanky Gregg Miller, who was also Hackenbush's current guitar player. That those two were still together after more than a year was rather amazing and mostly a tribute to Shorty's cherubic looks and hard-headed good sense that had won over and kept Gregg from living out his Keith Richard fantasies. On the other hand, if Gregg was living out those fantasies with Shorty, well, good for both of them.

"And there's Melanie Moreau," Arlo said, waving at a cool blond in a strapless number. "I saw her play Desdemona last year, she was brilliant. Y'think Vogler saw it? I doubt it."

Hackenbush shrugged and then froze. She'd just spotted someone she didn't like almost as much as she didn't like the person that person usually went to these kinds of parties with.

Following Hackenbush's piercing polar gaze, Arlo said, "And there's Mimi Buk. I heard her read some of her poetry a few weeks ago. She's, ah, getting better... I think."

Hackenbush began to scan the crowd.

"And it's not just the poetry thing," Arlo continued. "It's the performance thing."

"Don't say it," Hackenbush gritted out, looking around her for a quick exit. She'd never make it over the wrought iron fence in that dress.

"No, really, Hackenbush, the line between performance art–"

Hackenbush winced hard.

"–and readings–"

"Arlo, stop!"

"–gets blurrier every day."

"No! Arlo! No! Stop!" she hissed furiously.

"Let's face it, Hackenbush–"

"Let's not!" Her skin was starting to crawl.

"–the most misunderstood person in any gathering of non-felons is always going to be–"

"No, Arlo, no! Don't say it! Don't! Say! Her! Name!"

"–Ana Phalaxia."

A gaunt, smirking wraith-like creature materialized from the shadows, or the hydrangea, behind them. Ana Phalaxia, blinking in the glare of the luminarias lining the garden path, stepped forward and fixed Hackenbush with her terrible eye. "I heard my name."

Arlo murmured, "Sorry, Hackenbush," and tried to slink away. He was firmly yanked back to her side.

Ana Phalaxia always looked like something the cat dragged in on a rainy night. And then dragged out again and tried to bury somewhere. Tonight she was all dressed up and, incredibly, looked even worse. As if summoned by dark arts or the smell of her master's corruption, Phalaxia's protégée and hench-poet Mimi Buk joined them. As they arranged themselves to cut off any escape, Ana smiled at Mimi and turned back to her helpless victims. "Now, what were you two conventional artists talking about?" she asked sweetly. It was horrible, and 'conventional artist' was a pretty serious insult from her.

Squaring his shoulders, Arlo was going to be brave, but Hackenbush saved him the trouble.

"We were talking about that genius in the Bay Area, J.F. Elouardio," she said. "Certainly you've heard of him, Ana, even if you don't read 'The Secret Alameda' magazine on a regular basis."

"Perhaps," Ana drawled. "I hear of so many things. What does this Ernesto–"

"Elouardio," Arlo said helpfully. He wasn't sure where Hackenbush was going with his idol, J.F., but he at least wanted Phalaxia to get his name right before Hackenbush slammed her into the ground.

"J.F. Elouardio is one of the greatest artists evah," Hackenbush drawled at Phalaxia. Hackenbush was a girl who got a lot out of a long 'a' sound. "He makes acrylics look like oils, oils look like enamels, his collages make grown men cry, and his assemblages, my dear Phalaxia, he'd have done a better job than God cobbling Adam together, if he'd been around, and certainly J.F. would have made an even better Eve. One that could fly, control her fertility, and photosynthesize her own food."

"I see," Ana folded her arms and narrowed her eyes.

Mimi and Arlo took surreptitious steps to get behind their respective dates.

"But J.F. has left us all even further in the dust, Ana," Hackenbush declaimed. "He makes insects of us all."

"Oh? How so?" Phalaxia asked coldly. She knew she looked a little like a Praying Mantis, but never liked being reminded of it.

"Well, I'll tell you: J.F. Elouardio is making art in his head," Hackenbush fixed Phalaxia with her own terrible eye. "And leaving it there."

Phalaxia was a pretty good sport, at least when Hackenbush had her on the ropes. There was no way to call the singer a liar without starting World War III, and, if she let herself enjoy it, Hackenbush had just spun her a pretty good yarn. "I see," she said, almost pleasantly. "How... exclusive. Is he selling well?"

"Feh, yes, but that hardly matters to such a genius."

"He must have excellent representation," Ana said, and figured she better change the subject before Hackenbush launched into some neurological explanation of neocortical art sales. "Speaking of fine artists, I mean the kind who let their work out of their heads," she said over Hackenbush's shoulder to Arlo. "I saw your teacher, Davido, here earlier."

"Really? I'm surprised. He said he'd see Vogler in hell before he'd copy that painting," Arlo said. "I only did it because ELAG twisted my arm."

"Well, you did learn to draw there," Hackenbush said tartly. "And paint, and sculpt, and write grants, and—"

"Yes. I know." Arlo scowled at Hackenbush's sarcastic frown and then at Phalaxia's louche smirk. "Is he still here?"

"Davido?" Phalaxia asked. "I haven't seen him since I saw him talking with someone behind the caterer's tent. He wasn't in fancy dress, so I don't image he was planning to stay."

"Huh. That's surprising..." Arlo was frowning now.

"Arlo! Come with me!" A muscular woman with short hair grabbed the painter and dragged him toward the house.

"Who was that?" Mimi asked.

Hackenbush and Phalaxia jumped; they'd forgotten she was there. "I've no idea," Phalaxia told her protégée. "Hackenbush?"

Hackenbush sighed. "That was Pam Tucker. Good painter, no manners whatsoever."

"Is she one of the copyists?" Phalaxia asked.

"Yeah, don't be cruel, Ana; those twelve poor bastards put aside everything they hold sacred to help ELAG," she said. "I salute them."

"As do I, Hackenbush, as do I," Phalaxia murmured. "But I also understand why Davido didn't cave in."

"He's too big and arrogant? Try again, Ana, he hasn't sold anything in years," Hackenbush snarled. "I hear he's living on his ego and handouts from his students. He's washed up."

"That's not entirely wrong, but not what I was going to say," Phalaxia said with an edge to her voice. "Davido didn't cut his art teeth at ELAG; he's got no loyalty to it."

"Especially when many of the ELAG kiddies went on to study with him and then left him in the dust," Hackenbush said. "No, no reason for Davido to care about ELAG a't'all a't'all."

"Please don't quote Hobo Kelly to me," Phalaxia said. "My little sisters watched that show until I wanted to kill them all."

"Too bad for you, Ana. By the way, where did you get that dress?" Hackenbush asked, recoiling slightly from the rag just barely covering Phalaxia's ectomorph frame.

"I found it in the gutter at 9th and Olympic."

"Ah, the Fashion District. Did you wash it?"

"No."

"Pam, please, go easy on the monkey suit," Arlo said as he was dragged along by a lapel. "You're bruising the polyester."

"This is bigger than your wardrobe, Arlo." Pam was a woman of few words except when she needed more than a few. This was almost one of those times: "Fuck, shit, fuck!"

"What? What? What?" Arlo looked around the huge drawing room and the people milling around in it. It looked normal to him: The Siqueiros was over the fireplace and there were six copies on either side of it. All the furniture had been removed for the evening, so there was only a lectern for the auctioneer and rows of seats for the bidders. Arlo slumped a little; the fucking auction was going to be the worst part—what if his copy didn't sell for the most? How would he ever live it down?

"There are too many civilians in this room."

Arlo turned his head to look at her, she was staring a hole in the Siqueiros. He almost felt sorry for it. "Why is–?"

"Wait here." Pam dashed off the way she'd come. She ran back to where she'd last seen Ana Phalaxia. "Ana Phalaxia! That's you, right? I need you!"

"Go for it, Pam!" Hackenbush said, making a hasty exit from the scene. "I'd never put those last three words together with Phalaxia, but you're a braver woman than I," she added over her shoulder.

"Pam Tucker, isn't it?" Phalaxia asked, ready for a fight. She'd really had enough of Hackenbush's sass and had been about to put the little vocalist in her place. "Have we met?"

"No."

"Oh."

"I need a diversion." Pam smiled evilly. "I hear you give good diversion."

"Well, I don't usually take requests, but..." Phalaxia leaned forward to hear Pam's spiel, while watching Renee Soleil cross the patio far away from Hackenbush, who was also crossing the patio. Luckily it was a big patio.

Hackenbush had been badly in need of a drink and a rescue from Phalaxia. There was only so much of the woman she could take and she'd nearly reached her limit when Pam, wonderful Pam! had come to her rescue. She flagged down a waiter, who was delighted to give her a glass of champagne.

It was taking more cool than the usual Hackenbushian cool to watch the Eddy Lee Trio do fine and beautiful things with "Girl From Ipanema." Eddy was looking mighty fine when he was looking at her, and scruffy, rumpled, and seriously in need of a shampoo and blow dry when he was looking at someone else, especially when that person was Renee Soleil. As usual he was playing like some kind of guitar god, but that was the very least one could expect from Eddy Lee.

Renee Soleil was another matter, now; there was undeniably a whole lot of woman and an amazing singer under all the fat. If Hackenbush had any competition in LA, it was Renee. Fortunately Hackenbush and the band, including Shorty, currently had one of the best gigs in town at the newly renovated Lotus Room at the Hotel Watanabe in Little Tokyo. This was good; it meant Hackenbush could be benevolent and let Renee have the other good jobs in town. If she was completely honest with herself, Renee was almost as good a singer as she was. She didn't have to be honest about how well she'd do in a catfight with Renee, who outweighed her by at least thirty pounds. In that kind of situation, Hackenbush's only hope was to outrun the bitch, something she was fairly certain she could do even in a tight skirt and high heels.

The Jobim tune came to an end and received the usual polite applause. The applause got louder as a striking lady with blond hair and powerful features stepped up to the microphone. She was dressed very simply and elegantly and spoke with confidence. She introduced herself as Manuela Alonso y Sierra, the new director of ELAG. She graciously thanked everyone for coming to the fundraiser, thanked the artists, thanked the Vogler family, and said wonderful things about Los Angeles.

"I thank you all for a gracious welcome to your city," she said. "I know I will be very happy in my new home in Los Angeles." There was a decent wave of applause. "And I understand from my dear friend, Ana Phalaxia," more applause (but less enthusiastic)," that we are lucky tonight to have two of the greatest singers in Los Angeles with us tonight. Renee Soleil and Dr. Hackenbush!" She paused to acknowledge the polite applause, and then she dropped a bombshell: "It is my dearest hope that perhaps we could have both of these artists sing for us tonight. Together on the same stage, as Ana says this has never occurred before in musical history. Ana tells me this cannot be done, but tonight is a magical night, and I think anything can happen!"

There was more lukewarm applause. Probably most of this crowd didn't know either singer; this might have been to moment to feign throat problems and graciously back out of the performance. Hackenbush caught Renee's eye across the patio, and they stared at each other with polite smiles, both of them trying to figure a way out of this goddam horrible goddam idea goddam Phalaxia had goddam dreamed up.

However bad Renee and Hackenbush looked at that moment, Eddy Lee looked worse: he looked like he was looking into the jaws of hell. Maybe he was, but even Eddy knew when he had to be a gentleman and not let a lady, even one as clueless this Sierra woman, down.

Wearing his Gibson hollow body guitar like a shield against all evil, he stepped up to the microphone.

"Ladies and gentlemen, Ms. Sierra is correct," he said. "If you would be so kind as to welcome the one, the only, Miss Renee Soleil!" He and Sierra led the applause until Renee really had no choice but to head for the stage. "And, direct from the middle class, the fabulous Dr. Hackenbush!"

"Well, at least he got the intro right," Hackenbush thought. "Good thing I'm a lady, an artist, a good sport, and a much better singer than Renee. Oh, dear God, what are we supposed to sing together?" She passed close enough to Phalaxia to fry any normal person with her glare, but the creature merely waggled her bushy eyebrow at her. The uni-brow was in vogue that year, but Phalaxia, always so far ahead of the curve as to be in orbit, had had hers for decades.

"Well, Hackenbush," Renee said coolly. "Here we are."

"Yes, well, yes. This just proves nothing is impossible, don't it?"

"Oh, yes! What shall we sing?"

"I was just wondering about that."

"Why don't you sing that song from "Annie Get Your Gun," Mimi Buk yelled helpfully. "You know, the one about anything you can do, I can do better?"

"A show tune, Mimi? You want us to do a show tune?" Hackenbush asked over the applause, trying to get some real horror into her voice.

"Don't you know it, Mabel?" Renee said sweetly. Rather unhelpfully Eddy's bass player had the bad taste to play the first line for them.

Hackenbush turned her head a fraction of an inch toward her rival and, at the moment, co-star. "Of course I know it, Renee," she said, equally sweetly. "I thought you might prefer something more along the lines of, oh, I don't know, the "Love Boat" theme."

Renee trilled her annoying fake laugh. "Oh dear, no, I like Mimi's suggestion," she said way too pleasantly and stepped closer to the single microphone. "Ed?" she asked

"Yeah, Ed?" Hackenbush asked. She joined Renee in front of the solitary mike. Not too close; they'd both have to sing loud to be heard, but it was only one song in what they figured would be long careers and it would not kill them. At least they hoped so.

"Wh-what key, girls?"

"G?" Hackenbush asked Renee.

"G is good."

And four bars of introduction later, they sounded like they'd been singing together for lifetimes.

"All right, children, what the hell is going on in here?" Sierra squared off with her twelve Siqueiros copyists, Phalaxia by her side.

"That Siqueiros is a fake," Pam said in a rush.

"Pam, there are twelve copies–"

"No, the one in the middle is supposed to be the original, and I'm telling you: it's a fake."

"How can you tell this, Ms. Tucker?" Phalaxia asked before it could turn into a shouting match.

"Because the goddam paint is still wet!" Pam shoved her smudged fingers in Phalaxia's face.

Sierra went up to the alleged fake for a closer look. "Oh shit."

Outside on the patio, Irving Berlin, western music, and civilization itself were getting a run for their money. Hackenbush and Soleil were taking "Anything You Can Do, I Can Do Better" apart, note by note, and putting it back together again. The Eddy Lee Trio was breaking its first sweat of the evening. They had their hands full laying down a cool foundation for two of the touchiest singers in town and staying the hell out of their way.

Lesser musicians would have been scorched to death already by a single glare from either Hackenbush or Soleil. There'd already been at least one hard look at the drummer, the youngest and most vulnerable of Eddy's trio, but he recovered and laid off the tam-tam. Even the squares were hep to the jive, if only subconsciously, as they relaxed into the hurricane of vocal prowess unleashed on them.

Whatever Phalaxia's nefarious plan had been, it was backfiring. Instead of bringing each other down, Hackenbush and Soleil were bringing the house down.

"So what do we do now?" Arlo asked.

"Maybe there's a good explanation," Sierra said, pacing the hearth rug.

"Like what?" Pam asked. "Somebody stole the real one and put a fake in its place?"

Sierra looked like someone had hit her with a baseball bat.

"So what do we do now?" Arlo asked again.

"Where's Mr. Vogler?" Phalaxia asked. "It's his painting."

"Wait! Not yet!" Sierra grabbed Phalaxia by the shoulders. "Can't we tell him after the auction?"

They all thought about this for a while, and Pam spoke up: "And then we explain to the cops why we knew before the auction, but didn't call them until afterwards?"

"Bad idea," Phalaxia said, patting Sierra's clenched hands, trying to get them off her shoulders before she crushed a rotator cuff.

"So what do we do now?" Arlo asked. Even he was getting bored with the question.

Sierra sighed and let her hands drop to her sides. "I'll go get Mr. Vogler," she said, and left the room.

"Thanks for the distraction, Ms. Phalaxia," Pam said in the ensuing uncomfortable silence. "Hackenbush and Renee sound good together."

"Yes." Phalaxia scowled. "Shocking, isn't it?"

"Guy and Dolls" didn't need any horns; it had Hackenbush and Soleil. Hackenbush's voice had been compared to Eric Dolphy's alto sax. Renee's voice had the punch and clarity of a trumpet, slightly dark, but not smoky enough to be a flugelhorn. Eddy Lee exchanged a wry look with his bassist under an elegant run by Hackenbush. They braced for Renee's reply, which would either be more ornate or less complicated, which would out-cool Hackenbush's chromaticism. Either way, Eddy and his boys and all the jazz musicians in the audience would have a lot to think about and work into their own ideas of this tune.

"You must be joking, Ms. Sierra." Mr. Vogler stood in front of thirteen copies of his painting.

"No," Sierra said, going up on tiptoe and taking the painting down. She turned it over. "This is new wood and new canvas." She looked at her left palm. "And wet paint."

Vogler stared at Sierra's hand for a moment. Arlo, Pam, Sierra, and Phalaxia stared at him. "I'll call the police," he finally said, and left the room.

"Body and Soul." Renee announced this like a challenge.

It was; "Body and Soul" was a tune very close to Hackenbush's heart and Hackenbush had a moment of wanting to get her nails very close to Renee's eyes. "I might know that tune," she said coldly.

"You can sing a descant to it," Renee said.

"Just try to keep up, Renee." Hackenbush jerked her head at Eddy, who played the introduction he and Hackenbush had worked out when they were falling in love.

It was almost painful for him; the evening had

been going so well. He'd been ready for anything, except to be flung back six years and overwhelmed by all the happy memories he'd thrown away when he ran away from loving Hackenbush. Added to that was the piercing reminder of Renee's cruelty; she'd picked the one song that meant something to both Eddy and Hackenbush, which was also one of the best songs in Renee's repertoire, and the song Eddy could never bear to hear her sing. He wasn't so sure he could bear to hear Hackenbush sing it either; having to live through them both singing it at the same time was almost too much for a mere man, a guitar player at that, to endure.

But instead of using "Body and Soul" to tear each other apart, Renee and Hackenbush put all their hearts into making the song even more beautiful. Hackenbush set the mood by singing note for note the first eight bars of Coltrane's version of "Body and Soul," which she considered the ne plus ultra version of the tune. Then she and Renee proceeded to conjure lush harmonies and counterpoint out of thin air, using the tune's original structure only as a touchstone now and then. It was still "Body and Soul," but it was as if the singers had reached deep into the composer's mind for the ideas he never had time, or possibly the guts, to write. Eddy Lee put aside his awe, and rose to the occasion with a solo that inspired the singers even more. Finally coming back to earth, they sang the last sixteen bars in unison with the guitar, which was as close to heaven that those three ever got at the same time.

The applause might have been more thunderous except for two City of San Marino policemen crossing the patio interrupting it.

"Hey, hey, who called the riot squad?" Renee asked in an undertone.

"I knew we were swingin', Renee," Hackenbush undertoned back. "But I thought it was all legal."

The Vogler fortune began as orange and olive groves and then expanded exponentially as real estate. Their host, L. Vogler, was living off the proceeds of his father's and grandfather's hard work, the fortuitous locations of their groves, and impeccable timing. The last groves in Orange County were sold just as the area around the El Toro Marine base began residential development. The Voglers were not as well known as the Segerstrom family, nor as elegant as the Irvines or O'Neills. They were San Gabriel Valley snobs and couldn't care less about such a remote and sparely populated place as Orange County.

The current head of the Vogler family, art patron, and at the moment wondering what all the racket was on his patio, had bought the San Marino mansion after his father died on the last of the orchard property in the fifties. This Vogler hated getting his hands dirty; he was happy to sell what was left of the farms and move to what he considered civilization. Once there, he set about acquiring a fancy wife who left him as soon as she'd recovered from giving birth to their son, Emil. After hiring enough domestic help to raise his heir, Vogler threw himself back into social climbing. He was good at it, and even economical; he got the most bang for whatever buck he spent making himself look good. Although he didn't really understand multiculturalism, he'd put his support behind its institutions because doing so got him the most attention. He considered his charity the white man's burden, and helping a struggling barrio art school was easier than actually doing anything about racism, inequality, or injustice.

Vogler had been enjoying himself immensely at his own party, weird jazz singing notwithstanding, until Sierra had pulled him aside for a word. For a big man, he could move quickly when called upon. He strode into the drawing room and was completely ignored by eleven of the artists who were puzzling over why Pam had seen the fake and they had not. Their self-esteems were too impacted to notice their host, until he got on a chair to look at "his" painting.

"Jesus, you'd think he owns the place," muttered one of the artists.

"He does," Phalaxia told her, and smiled her marrow-chilling smile. It was unnecessary to smile like that, but she hadn't freaked anyone out in twenty minutes and was craving it. It was most effective; the poor devil moved off in a hurry.

"You're quite right, Manuela, this is not my painting." he said, wiping the paint off his hands; he was looking very annoyed as he went off to call the police.

He got even frownier when the police arrived to make a report and he had to tell all his guests they couldn't leave until they'd given their contact information to the officers.

"Well, this is annoying," Hackenbush said to Shorty. Like anyone but a pillar of society or a super criminal, talking to the police made her nervous. She accepted another glass of champagne from a passing waiter, and even the waiter looked slightly annoyed. It had been a long night for the servers already. Hackenbush hoped their host, (Mr. Vulgar? Volger? No! Vogler!) was a good tipper.

Shorty nodded. He wasn't too thrilled either. Not that he had anything to hide, but uniforms creeped him out and made him giggle in what lesser minds might consider a guilty fashion. "You sounded good up there, dearie," he said to distract himself from his nervousness.

"With Renee? Yeah, kind of scary, weren't it?"

He smirked at her. She knew she sounded good, she always sounded good, no matter what she might feel. Shorty caught Eddy's eye and pantomimed a two-step. He got a wink and a pretty good view of Eddy's aging profile as he leaned back to talk to his drummer and bassist. Well, they were all getting older; dating a man in his early 20s brought that home to Shorty every time he and Gregg had a conversation.  Good thing they had art and music and sex to keep them together, good thing those were enough, because otherwise they just didn't have much common ground to stand around and look cool on.  "Let's dance, Mabel," he said, more order than request, when Eddy glided his Gibson into "Moonglow."

"Ah, the bastard could always play that song, couldn't he?" she asked as Shorty guided her onto the makeshift dance floor.

They weren't there to put on a show, just let off a little nervousness.  Quite of a few other guests must have had the same yen because pretty soon the dance floor was like rush hour on the 110 Freeway through downtown.

"I'm surprised you and Gregg came to this mess," Hackenbush said as they were taking a breather from the crush of the dance floor.  She lit a Pall Mall and picked a shred of tobacco off her tongue.  "I heard you ran into Eddy Lee at Pipers last week and called him a prick."

"He was with Janet Tran and that pissed me off," Shorty said.  He was blunt with Hackenbush because if he jerked her around she'd use something blunt on his tender flesh.  "I think if Eddy's going to throw himself away, dearie, it behooves him to do it with someone who isn't practically engaged to someone else."

"Did you really use the word 'behooves'?" Hackenbush asked and just stared at him when he nodded.  "I must be tired to be so impressed," she continued when Shorty didn't go on.  "Why do you care what Eddy does?"

"Because you do."

"Hah.  I've been on that ride," she said coldly. "I'm through with it."

"Says you," he said.  "I heard you tonight, you don't sound like that anywhere but when you're singing with Eddy."

"I was musically kicking Renee's ass."

"To impress Eddy."

"I think it behooves me to change the subject," she said, but found it wasn't so easy to swerve onto a completely new topic. "What did Gregg think of my performance?"

"He thinks you were trying to impress Eddy, too." Shorty weathered a withering stare. "But whenever Eddy shows up somewhere Gregg's playing, Gregg tries to impress him, too."

Hackenbush sighed out a lungful of smoke. "What is this strange power Eddy Lee has over us?"

"I wouldn't know, it doesn't affect me," Shorty said primly. "He's got bad taste in women–"

"Oh, fucking thank you!"

"–lately. I don't like Janet, I think she's trouble and I wish she'd leave us all alone," Shorty went on. "She wants to swan around high society with the Vogler types and slum with Eddy Lee. It ain't right, her using everyone that comes near her."

"I don't know her," Hackenbush said, eyeing a police officer taking names in the crowd. "Is she a cunt?"

"More of a black hole," Shorty said matter-of-factly. "She sucks the life out of everything she touches. Isn't that what black holes do?"

Hackenbush leaned close to Shorty's shell-like ear, and whispered: "Maybe she can suck the chrome off a Ford bumper and that's why Eddy's with her." She leaned back to watch Shorty writhe with suppressed laughter that nearly killed him, and had a hearty chuckle about it herself.

Fortunately they had pulled themselves together by the time the police officer came to ask their names, addresses, phone numbers, why they were at the party, and if they had noticed anything suspicious. They said, "No, nothing suspicious," and were just very glad he didn't ask if they'd noticed anything annoying or bizarre, because both of those adjectives could be summed up in the words "Ana Phalaxia," but would have taken all night to explain.

The cops got through the party guests, but Hackenbush was marooned waiting for them to get though with the artists. She always left with who brung her, even though she drove that night, so she could only smile and act nice as she paced the patio waiting for Arlo Mega's liberation. Even the band was packed up and on their way.

"Hey, Mabel."

She didn't run or scream or slap Eddy's face; she just turned around and smiled neutrally. "Yeah?"

"Need a ride somewhere?"

"Nah, I gotta drive Arlo home," she said, evading the guitar case he was swinging nervously. "When he got to my place earlier, he was so freaked out about this party, I decided to drive us. The cops are taking their time in there. He'll be in worse shape when he gets out." She jerked her chin at the cop-and-artists infested drawing room.

"Yeah... yeah, um, are you dating Arlo?"

"I'm his date tonight," she said, dodging the question while she wondered what the fuck it was to Eddy. "What's up with you and Janet Tran?"

He laughed and whistled a few bars of "Just a Gigolo."

"Yeah, right, Ed, and I'm Nancy Reagan," she said. "Where is Janet anyway? I thought this was her party, sort of."

"Dunno, I saw her earlier." Eddy decided not to mention the last time he saw Janet, she was taking pictures of the Hackenbush and Soleil vocal summit.

"She must have left before the cops sealed the joint off." Hackenbush accepted a Pall Mall from Eddy. "Thanks," she murmured as he lit it for her. "You don't have to wait with me, Ed."

"No, I wanted to talk to you, Mabel," he said sincerely (for him). "I never see you alone."

"We're both busy, Ed," she said, leaving out the

"you could fucking call me" part of the sentence.

"That was kind of cool, y'know, earlier."

"Me and Renee."

"Yeah."

"Goddam Phalaxia."

"I liked it!" Phalaxia said, suddenly right next to her.

Hackenbush nearly jumped into Eddy's arms when Phalaxia materialized next to her. "Fuck, Ana, how do you do that?"

"Do what?" Phalaxia just stared at them when they didn't answer. "Quite a performance tonight. I didn't think you had it in you anymore, Mabel."

Eddy laid a restraining hand on his ex-fiancée.

"And then the police," Phalaxia went on. "So much stress, so much tension."

"Ana, what the fuck are you still doing here?" Hackenbush asked when she could.

"I'm soaking up the atmosphere," she said. "I might use it in a show I'm thinking of."

"Show about what?" Eddy asked.

"Misery."

"Ah, misery, good subject." Hackenbush waved Arlo over. He looked exhausted and was carrying his copy of the Siqueiros. "Are you taking it home?" she asked.

"Yeah, no auction, no sale."

"Sorry, Arlo," she said. "Can we go?"

"Yes, let's go." Arlo took her arm and said, "Hello, we must be going," to Eddy and Ana, and split with Hackenbush.

"Well, 'night, Ana," Eddy said after Hackenbush and Arlo were out of sight.

"Eddy, where's Janet?" she asked.

"I dunno, I don't have her on a leash," he said. "Well, 'night."

"The police were asking," Ana went on. "And

they were asking about Emil, too."

"They don't check in with me, Ana," Eddy said, annoyed. "Well, I gotta–"

"How well do you know Janet?"

"Right now I wish didn't know her at all!"

"That's not really an answer, Ed." Ana folded her arms and narrowed her eyes at him.

"Look, Ana, I nailed her a couple of times for fun and then it wasn't so much fun anymore," Eddy was pissed off enough to say. "She's a selfish little art babe who doesn't know what she wants from one minute to the next, so she wants everything she can grab onto. Good enough?"

"Yes, Ed, thank you."

"Bye, Ana." He turned to go and then turned back. "Um, look, I know you were making trouble tonight for Hackenbush and Renee, but, ah..."

Ana raised her mono-brow at him.

"...but, thanks." Eddy picked up his guitar and his amp, and headed for his car. It'd been a long night for him, but when all was said and done, a good one.

"How'd it go with the cops, Arlo?" Hackenbush asked as they headed down Mission toward her place in Lincoln Heights. "They kept y'all kind of a long time."

"Woulda gone faster if Miss Cuban Lady had gotten out of the white cops' faces. We'd've been done if she'd stopped arguing about everyone's constitutional rights."

"Well, the lady doesn't have a problem with authority," Hackenbush said.

"Yes, she does. She doesn't know when to back off," he said, tired and bitter. "Sometimes that's worse than backing down."

"Maybe she was just trying to protect–"

Arlo cut her off. "Nah, she's just a bi– she's just got a strong personality." He sighed, as much from tiredness as frustration. "She's ruffling a lot of feathers at ELAG, too. The first show she's going to curate there is for an African American artist."

"So?"

"Well, ELAG fancies itself the center of Chicano culture and–"

Hackenbush cut him off. "Oh yeah? I thought ELAG had a rainbow-color-blind-coalition-art-for-everyone kind of philosophy."

"They used to, Hackenbush, they're a little more exclusive these days."

The penny finally dropped. "Ah, racism," Hackenbush observed. "Oh, don't get me wrong, Arlo," she went on after his annoyed grunt. "I think Los Angeles has reached an almost utopian equilibrium of racism. It's a very unique accomplishment. I guess I thought ELAG was above all that."

"It was, Hackenbush, and it will be again."

They were quiet until they got to Chez Hackenbush. "Wanna come in, Arlo?"

"For a cup of coffee?"

"Nah," she said. "It'd keep you awake. I'll make you one in the morning."

It took him a moment, but then he figured it out. "One of us has bad timing, Mabel," he said. "I'm too tired and too pissed off to come in tonight." He leaned over and kissed her on the cheek. "But I will not forget this."

Hackenbush laughed and they got out of her car. Ever the gentleman, Arlo waited until she was in the house with the door closed before he drove off. "Just my luck," he thought. But he knew better to start something with Hackenbush that he couldn't start well. He knew her well enough to know she'd hate him if he was unsure of himself or took advantage of what he strongly suspected was an Eddy Lee induced Hackenbushian moment of weakness, so it was better to be strong enough to just say no...for now.

"Well that was bold of me," Hackenbush thought as she put her evening gown away. "I guess I need more practice coming on to guys who seem to want me to." She was so distracted by her failed seduction, she didn't notice until the next day that Arlo had left his Siqueiros copy in the tiny backseat of her Karmann Ghia. Knowing an oil painting was one of the least destructible things in the world, she put it in the trunk, planning to return it at her earliest convenience. Had it been a photograph or a print or something that warps in heat and cold, she would have taken it inside. But oil paintings are tough, which makes them worth the effort that goes into them.

A few days later Arlo strolled into the Lotus Room to catch the last of *Dr. Hackenbush and her Orchestra*'s last set. One look from the diva told him he should have shelled out for a dozen of her favorite yellow roses to cover for the fact he hadn't called, written or come in person since her come-on the other night. Well, he'd been busy, very, very busy, which was why he was there.

It was the very last song of the evening, "Look for the Silver Lining," the band's theme song, and after Hackenbush said good night, she carried her baritone ukulele over to Arlo's table. "May I join you?" she asked, ignoring the band and Shorty's staring at them.

"If it won't get me lynched, Mabel, sure," he said, rising to pull out a chair for her. "Sorry I haven't called or anything. The cops have been all over me and the other painters."

"Why?"

"I guess you don't read the papers," he said. "Emil Vogler was shot during the party. They found him upstairs after we all left that night. The cops said he was shot with his own gun."

"Oh, Christ..."

"Yeah, ELAG hired a lawyer to help us," he said. "It's the artists they're focusing on."

"What about Janet?" she asked.

"Janet who?"

"Janet Tran, she's, I mean, she was Emil Vogler's girlfriend," Hackenbush said, and then scowled. "I even got a call from- from someone asking about her."

"I don't know nothin' about Janet," Arlo said. "Who called you?"

Hackenbush looked around nervously and then whispered, "Phalaxia. If I say her name too loud–"

"Yeah, what a pest," Arlo snapped. "She's in the Ladies Room freshening up and making a phone call. She's the one who dragged me in here."

"Really?"

"Yeah, she fucking shows up at my studio and won't leave until I give her Davido's address," Arlo fumed. "I brought her here to stall. Help me out, Mabel."

"With Phalaxia?" Hackenbush asked.

"Right here," Phalaxia said, causing them to jump. "How do I get a drink around here?"

"Uh, you get a cab and go to the Bonaventure," Hackenbush said. "They have drinks and snacks there."

As if to make a liar of her, Wang the bartender plonked down a bowl of pretzels and took their drink orders. The band finished at one but the bar was open until two. It wasn't unusual for Hackenbush to sit with friends until last call.

"Well, anyway, Hackenbush, you might get hauled in for more questioning," Arlo said, picking up the conversation some ways back. "Just a heads up."

"Hackenbush, have you seen Janet?" Phalaxia dove in.

"No."

"Have you heard from Eddy Lee?"

"Hell no."

Phalaxia flagged down the band's drummer, who shared a house in mid-Wilshire with Eddy. "Ross, has Eddy seen Janet Tran?" she asked.

"How the fuck would I know?" he asked. He sketched Hackenbush and Arlo a wave and was gone. Hackenbush watched him go; Ross was a fine looking man from behind. She thought he looked like the back of Paul Robeson that night.

"Did you tell the cops about seeing Davido before the party?" Hackenbush asked, aping Phalaxia's interrogatory stylings.

"No."

"Did you ask them to look for Janet?"

"No."

"Why not? You're looking for both of them," Hackenbush said. "The cops are better at this than you are. Unless..."

Phalaxia just stared at her.

"Unless what?" Arlo asked, unable to bear the suspense.

"Unless you're protecting them," Hackenbush said to Phalaxia.

"From the cops? Of course," Phalaxia said with a snort.

"It's a murder, Phalaxia," Hackenbush said.

"Neither of them are killers," she said. "At least Janet isn't. What about Davido, Arlo?"

"Nah, not with a gun anyway," Arlo said after thinking it over for a moment. "Nah, he's more of the ax-murder type."

The women stared at him. "I tried to call Davido again," Phalaxia said at last. "Still no answer."

"He might have a date," Arlo said. "He has a life, you know."

"I've been trying to call for three days, Arlo," Phalaxia gritted out. "Does he have dates for three days?"

Arlo shrugged.

"Let's go, Arlo," Hackenbush said, suddenly all resolve and curiosity.

"Okay! Your place or mine?!"

Phalaxia's mono-brow hit her hairline.

"Davido's," Hackenbush said, gathering her stuff up. "I'll follow you there. Oh, and I have your picture."

"I was hoping I left it in your car," he said, resignedly heading for the parking garage. The only thing that made him a little less bitter at being bullied like this was that Hackenbush told the bartender to put their drinks on her tab.

Once in the parking garage, Hackenbush was horrified when Phalaxia got in the car with her. "Um, Phalaxia, why don't you–"

"Don't lose him, Hackenbush," Phalaxia said, waving at the taillights on Arlo's truck.

Hackenbush sighed and did as she was told. She wasn't too hip on this goose chase, but it seemed like the only way to rescue Arlo from the Phalaxia. She figured he was worth it. "Oh, shit, I didn't give him his picture."

"He'll get it later." Phalaxia relaxed into her seat as much as it's ever possible to relax into a vintage VW seat. "What's going on with you two?"

"Me and Arlo? Nothing."

"Yet."

"Mind your own fucking business, Phalaxia."

"How about you and Eddy Lee?"

"Less than nothing," Hackenbush admitted. "It was, y'know, fun to sing with him again."

"Even if you had to share the stage with Renee."

"I hate to ruin your fun, sugar, but once I got into it, I actually enjoyed it," Hackenbush said grimly. "I guess there was no other way it could have happened. Too bad nobody was taping it."

"I saw Janet snapping a few pictures."

"Is that why you're looking for her?" Hackenbush asked. "Evidence of your wickedness?"

Phalaxia was quiet for longer than usual. "I'm worried about her," she finally said. "Emil was murdered. They were practically engaged. She shouldn't have disappeared like that."

"Maybe Janet stole the painting," Hackenbush ventured.

"Why? Janet organized that party and fundraiser," Phalaxia said. "She's a climber, and a jerk, and not a very good photographer, but why would she wreck a chance to get a little higher on the LA art food chain? She's not that stupid."

"She's fucking Eddy Lee, she can't be that bright," Hackenbush said, and instantly regretted it. "I mean–"

"I know what you mean."

"No, you don't," she said, suddenly very tired of the whole subject. "I mean Janet was practically engaged to a rich guy's son. Why throw that away on anybody? Least of all Eddy? If she needed a back-up lay, why not get someone hotter and richer? I hear they're out there, in Redondo Beach or places like that."

"There's nothing wrong with Eddy," Phalaxia said, abstractedly.

"I didn't say there was."

"There might be some purity in sleeping with a failure–"

"He's not a failure."

"He's not exactly a success, Hackenbush," Phalaxia said. "He can't even get you back and you still love him."

"No, I don't."

"Then you respect him as an artist. That's even better than love. I think we're here."

Davido's studio was off Fletcher Drive in the ancient commercial area behind the Van de Kamp bakery south of Glendale. Technically it was at the extreme edge of LA, but it was so deserted, it felt like nowhere. There were no artist's lofts there, only decrepit buildings that rented a lot of space for cheap, if you didn't mind rats, roaches, and dodgy plumbing. Davido had had his studio there for a long time, but he'd been on the skids for a long time, too.

It was very dark in the alley and no lights on in the studio. Arlo knocked quietly on the door and called out for his old mentor. No answer. "Nobody home, let's go," he said, cheerfully.

"Knock harder, please," Phalaxia said, planting herself in front of him.

He knocked harder. No answer. "Let's go."

Phalaxia marched up to the door and tried the knob. It was open. She took a step back from it.

"At this hour in this neighborhood?" Hackenbush murmured, glancing up and down the deserted alley. "That can't be good."

Arlo frowned. "He'd never leave his door unlocked," he said. He pushed the door open and called Davido's name. Hackenbush hung back, but Phalaxia followed him inside, and then shrieked when Arlo found a light and turned it on. "Don't come in, Mabel!" he yelled.

She wasn't about to; she was rooted to the spot. Through the open door, she could see a pair of legs splayed out and dark stains around them.

Unfortunately they were in LA, but the Northeast precinct cops were okay. They and the morgue took their time taking Davido's body away, but they didn't grill Arlo or Phalaxia very much. They didn't grill Hackenbush at all because Phalaxia sent her home before the cops got there.

Every day after that night, Hackenbush expected either a call or a visit from the police. Neither came; she figured Arlo and Phalaxia must have nerves of steel. No one called her about Emil Vogler's murder either. This caused her to wonder just how much actual investigating the police were doing. On the other hand, there were dozens of people at that party; maybe the cops just hadn't gotten to her yet. Or maybe they had it solved. That was what she hoped, but figured someone would have told her by now if it was true.

When Arlo finally did call her, it was to invite her to a big meeting at ELAG the next night. Hackenbush had to work that night, but could come for at least the beginning of the meeting. "Do the ELAG people know I was with you when you found Davido?" she asked.

"I've wiped that fact from my mind, Hackenbush," he said. "Unless Phalaxia told them, and she's zipped pretty tight for a confessional performance artist."

Hackenbush laughed and said she'd see him there. She'd be along as soon as eastbound rush-hour traffic would allow.

She was late and wound up sitting in the back next to Eddy Lee, who must have also been late. Renee must have been on time because she was sitting near the front of the crowd. She was all gussied up, too, which meant she had a gig that night as well. "I can't believe you're not gigging tonight," Hackenbush said softly as Ms. Sierra recapped the party and the theft.

"I am working tonight," Eddy said.

Hackenbush gave him the once over: greasy hair, worn-out t-shirt, raggedy jeans and scuffed-up sneakers. "You're working like that?" she asked, immaculate in her cocktail dress, pumps and tasteful make-up.

"Well, excuse me, Miss Chi-Chi Downtown Lounge singer," he said with mock umbrage. "I'm playin' a blues gig in Venice later. Y'mind?"

Eddy was a really good blues guitarist when he got to be one. He'd traded grit for grace, not to mention steady money, with *Dr. Hackenbush and her Orchestra*, and Hackenbush always felt kind of bad about that. "I guess the only thing I mind is that I won't get to hear you," she said, not looking at him.

The silence got tight as he stared at her profile. "Mabel, I–"

"My name is Hector de la Vega and I am an attorney who has volunteered my time to help anyone being harassed by the police in this matter."

Hackenbush and Lee jumped to attention when the translator boomed this message to the crowd.

"Thank you for your attention," the translator added as Mr. de la Vega sat down.

A middle aged Chicano got up. He was dressed in jeans and a work shirt and Sierra introduced him as Juan Aguilar. Hackenbush sat up and took notice. Eddy leaned close, "Isn't that the guy...?"

"Yeah, the outsider-former-street-kid who almost won the council seat in the last election," Hackenbush said. "Got lots of press, but his old gang connections killed his chances. If you can believe what they print in the LA Times."

"But isn't he...?"

"Yeah, he's a youth counselor," she said, recalling a stellar profile of him as "The Great Brown Hope" in the LA Reader. "He's tryin' to get kids out of gangs. Figures if he could get out, anyone could. But nobody noticed that, just that he did some time in juvenile hall for some gang thing twenty years ago." Some people nearby shushed her and she shut up. Mr. Aguilar was speaking in English at that point.

"I can only tell you what the rumors are," he said. "My contacts say the painting was sold to an Ecuadorian lawyer named Enrique Morales in Quito, who thinks he's an art collector. Morales works for the Cali cartel, and can't come to the U.S. because the Drug Enforcement Agency wants to talk to him very much. Morales' people were supposed to pick up the painting after the party and fly it down to its new owner. As you know, that couldn't happen, and because nobody makes a fool of Enrique Morales, his people here, specifically a man named Tomas Rodriguez, have hired locals and out-of-towners to look for the painting and get it to Morales. Rodriquez negotiated the buy. It's a debt of honor for him now."

"Is that why my studio got tossed?" Pam asked.

"Probably. Rodriguez was at the party, he knows exactly who was there," Aguilar said blandly. "I hear he was especially impressed with the musical entertainment." He nodded at Renee, Hackenbush and Eddy Lee before turning back to Pam. "Just be glad you weren't in your studio when they were there, Miss..."

"Ms. Ms. Tucker." Pam nearly snapped at him. "They tore the place apart, too. And my copy wasn't even there. It's here, in Manuela's office."

Aguilar looked a question at Sierra, who stood up. "That's correct," she said. "Most of the paintings are here, but a few of the artists left before that decision was made." She sat down again.

"So, I guess if you have your painting," Aguilar went on in his relaxed tenor, "you should put it where it will be easy to find when your studio is broken into." He paused to let the panicky hubbub die down. "I can put the word out that most of the paintings are here, but I'm pretty sure Rodriguez's people will be very thorough."

"Can't the police–?" someone started to ask.

"No, they can't," Aguilar cut them off. "This is all rumor, gossip, innuendo. The police don't care, aren't interested and wouldn't listen. And what can they do anyway? Post a guard on all your studios?" He let that sink in for a moment. "The police have two murders to work on: one is Emil, but my sources say they think it was Janet Tran and so all their efforts are in looking for her. I hear that Emil was shot with his own gun; who else but his woman could get close enough to do that? At least that's what the police are thinking on that one."

Hackenbush glanced at Eddy, who'd stiffened beside her.

"My sources are pretty sure Rodriguez's people killed Davido," Aguilar went on. "No one knows why or how Davido was involved. He turned down the job, right?" he asked Sierra.

"Well, yes..." she said, looking at Phalaxia.

Phalaxia looked to her left at Arlo, who looked at Aguilar. "Um," Arlo said. "While we were waiting for the cops I saw a picture of the Siqueiros canvas over Davido's worktable."

"So? We all got a picture of the canvas, " Pam asked in the shocked silence.

"But you made a copy, Pam, and supposedly Davido did not," Phalaxia said dramatically. "We think Davido made the copy that replaced the original."

"How can you tell? Or how could you tell?" Aguilar asked.

"Well, you can't," Arlo said. "Davido was a master painter. His copy, if he made one, would be exactly like the original. I mean, except for the age of the canvas and bars–"

"And wet oils," Pam nearly snarled.

Arlo squinted at the scribbled note that had been handed to him. "'Fingerprints'?" he read, looking back at Hackenbush, who nodded vigorously.

Aguilar, Sierra and de la Vega had a quick conference. "Mr. de la Vega will bring all this up with the police tomorrow," Aguilar said. "Thank you, Mr., um..."

"Yeah, you're welcome," Arlo growled even though he was glad to be off the hot-seat. He gave Eddy and Hackenbush a hard look and decided he wasn't very happy seeing the two of them sitting together so amicably, but Aguilar was going on again.

"The other rumor is that the painting was donated to Mexico for their national museum, and this can be backed up," Aguilar said. He gestured to a trim young man in a suit sitting next to Sierra. "Mr. Acuna is the cultural attaché with the Mexican consulate here in Los Angeles. Perhaps you'd like to..."

"Yes, thank you, Mr. Aguilar," Mr. Acuna rose and addressed the crowd. He was relaxed and seemed comfortable speaking in public. "This is all so unfortunate. When Ms. Tran originally approached me with Mr. Vogler's generous–"

"Janet?!" Phalaxia yelled, leaping out of her seat. "Janet was going to give you–?"

"Ana, please!" Sierra stood up and so did everyone else.

In the ensuing melee Hackenbush said, "See ya, sugar," to Eddy Lee and split. She was in the parking garage at the New Hotel Watanabe when she remembered she'd forgotten to give Arlo his painting, which was still in her trunk. It was okay, she'd invite him over for dinner soon; he hadn't been looking too friendly at the meeting anyway. Or maybe he was just worried: having a bunch of thugs going from studio to studio looking for the Siqueiros and knowing it was just a matter of time before they got to his studio would make anyone look grumpy. Her heart went out to all the copyists, poor guys, and then her heart went into the very good pre-gig dinner the club gave her and the band. Halfway through the first set, she'd forgotten everyone's troubles, including her own.

Juan Aguilar was a realist and he knew his limitations. Even so, he was also a sucker for a good cause, lost or not, and he was still trying to figure out if that was a blessing or a curse. East Los Angeles Graphics was one of the best causes around, lost or otherwise, and Juan was doing his best for them. He just wished they'd called him in sooner because he would never had allowed them to get involved with the Vietnamese gangs in Little Saigon.

"Janet Tran is not a gang member," Phalaxia said in high dudgeon. "She's a photographer." She dragged the poor man to a wall with half a dozen of Janet's black and white prints in tasteful frames on it.

Juan looked very hard at the murky prints. "Okay, whatever you say," he said. "But she's no Manuel Alvarez Bravo."

"Few are, Juan, few are," Manuela said, putting several bags of take-out on the conference table. She'd been downstairs in the main gallery paying the delivery man. "Come and eat, you both look hungry." They looked wan and cranky, too, but she didn't say that.

"Manuela, what is this?" Juan asked, spooning up a tangle of cold, white noodles.

"Vietnamese food," she said, filling her own plate. "I thought it would fit the mood since we're here to talk about Janet."

"Gee, thanks, mija," he said, taking a little of everything. "I was in Garden Grove all day, eating this stuff, and getting nowhere with the gang liaisons down there."

"Your people wouldn't–?" Sierra started to ask.

"Oh, my fellow youth counselor and county social workers would love to help me," Juan said, getting more food. "It's the actual community that won't help. Those people are a wall."

Phalaxia laughed, or maybe choked a little; it was always hard to tell when she was laughing, especially when she was eating.

"What?" Juan asked.

"I don't know why you think Janet is in Little Saigon," Phalaxia said. "She was an émigré, but never a gang member."

"Was she one of the Boat People?" Manuela asked.

"I don't think so," Phalaxia said, wearily. "I tried to find some information, but the bastard Eddy Lee doesn't know anything that isn't X-rated about her. Or care for that matter."

"And why do you care so much?" Juan asked.

"If it's as bad as you say, Mr. Aguilar, then Janet is all alone in a very bad situation."

"All alone," he mocked. "She's got the whole fucking Vietnamese community sheltering her. If she could run for Governor tomorrow, she'd fucking win.

Christ, I wish I was Asian, those people are ruthless, organized and mobilized."

The women just stared at him, smiling grimly. It was no secret in LA that the goals and gains the African-Americans and Latinos worked so hard for benefited everyone, and this was not the case with the exclusionary and insular Asian and White communities, whose goals and gains only benefited themselves. "I never really thought about it until the advent of multiculturalism," Phalaxia said to get the conversation going again. "But being Asian is probably the way to go these days." She smiled creepily at her dinner companions. "Did you know that Nixon said somewhere on the tapes that he thought Black and Brown people were inferior to White people, but that Asians were superior to everyone."

"Nixon said that?" Juan asked and Phalaxia nodded. "Maybe I don't want to be Asian."

Phalaxia laughed or coughed (or both). "I've never been enamored of multiculturalism," she said. "It's always seemed too tribal to me. And White people don't have a tribe, just a culture. This must be the White man's new burden. Being excluded, being pushed to the margins, and getting to feel guilty about it, to boot."

"Ana, please, we're eating here," Manuela said. She winked at Juan, but he was too nonplussed to notice. "I like multiculturalism except when it becomes exclusionary and fragmented."

"Well, it's multiculturalism, not omniculturalism," Phalaxia said.

"Heh, omniculturalism," Juan said. "I like that. Maybe it will get there, but for now it's multiculturalism."

"Yes, and no one can get any arts grant funding in Los Angeles unless you're young, brown or dying of AIDS, which means gay and male, as well," Phalaxia said. "There are few good times to be a woman artist, White or not, these are worse than usual bad times."

"Ana!" Manuela yelled, looking apologetically at

Juan, who merely rolled his eyes. "But, you know, that's what Davido said."

"When?" Phalaxia asked.

"Oh, not to me, there was a rumor that he was a bitter–"

"No rumor, that was fact. But do go on."

"Thanks. Well, anyway, grant giving is a little like fashion," Manuela said. "There are fads; one only has to outwait them."

"And then there'll be another fad and another and none of them will be about the quality of the work," Phalaxia said, wearily. "Merely about whatever the fashion is at that moment. But artists don't make art to get funded or even to get love, we make art because we have it inside us and it's more painful not to make art than to be ignored. And if our work happens to move or enlighten someone, well, lucky them."

Manuela and Juan gazed at Phalaxia in her worn-out clothes and graying hair. Manuela had known Phalaxia for a long time, and had been influenced by her performances and writing even before they met. Juan just saw Phalaxia as an embittered burn-out, and he saw those all the time. "So, what did you find out, Juan?" Manuela asked.

"Me? Oh," he said. "I found out Janet was not one of the Boat People. Her poorer cousins were, and they brought whatever family over they could once they got settled in Garden Grove. The richer part of the family, the part Janet is from, was in Singapore or maybe Paris, and came over about eight or ten years ago, nobody knows for sure. Janet met Emil Vogler when they were USC students, and decided he was her best bet. Besides, a girl like Janet Tran would rather have a big house in Pasadena than work in the family business in Little Saigon any day. At least that's what the word on the street is."

"So why do you think they're protecting her?"

"Because she's still one of them, Manuela," Juan said. "And there are so many people looking for her, and she's disappeared so completely, where the fuck else could she be?"

"An excellent question. One we have all been asking." Although the voice from the doorway was smooth and urbane, the room temperature dropped about 10 degrees. "I am Tomas Rodriguez. I understand Juan has been talking to various people about this unfortunate matter–"

"We have a doorbell, Mr. Rodriguez," Manuela snapped.

Gliding into the light, Tomas Rodriguez looked the way he sounded; like a guy who was holding all the cards as well as a gun and a knife. "I did not notice," he said pleasantly. "Your door must have been unlocked, because my assistant opened it so easily." There were three or four people with him; they fanned out into the room around him.

Juan suppressed a shudder; he'd only met Rodriguez's street-level foot soldiers up to now. The boss was something else. The cost of his suit alone would have paid Juan's salary for six months, he probably spent more for a haircut than Juan spent on groceries, and the engraved cigarette case was probably platinum, not sterling. Mr. Rodriguez, with his JD from Loyola and his very limited law practice, was one of the most expensive and exclusive lawyers in Los Angeles. That is when he bothered to practice law; he'd figured out early that crime pays better than honest work, so he did crime. Elegant high-level financial crime that almost looked legal, and did it so well, very few people realized what a dangerous bastard he was.

"As I was saying." Rodriguez offered cigarettes, but only Ana took one. He lit it with a slim hi-tech looking lighter and looked the three at the table over like he was thinking of buying them (and deciding not to).

"This incident has caused far too many people too much embarrassment and discomfort. I understand you were in Little Saigon all day, Juan, did you find anything?"

"No," Juan said. "I didn't find Janet or any leads to her, if that's what you mean."

"A shame that one little girl and a valuable painting can disappear so completely." Rodriguez waved his cigarette around. "If she does have it, that is."

Manuela looked over her shoulder at her office. "Hey..."

"As long as we are here, Miss Sierra, my people will take a look around," Rodriguez said. He winced dramatically at the crash in another part of the studio and raised his voice, "Carefully look around."

"You know, Mr. Rodriguez, I've been wondering about something," Manuela said. She glared at Juan, who was trying to stare her into silence. "You bought that painting from Mr. Vogler, didn't you?"

"I did, on behalf of a friend and colleague."

"Then why did Vogler report it stolen?" she asked.

Rodriguez sighed and gave her a pitying look. "I don't know. Perhaps he wanted the insurance money."

"Ah," Manuela sighed. "That would make sense. Since you actually own the painting, do you suppose you could make Mr. Vogler withdraw the theft report? I mean, it's not really his property anymore, is it?"

"Ours was a private transaction."

"I'm sure it was," Manuela said quickly. "But as long as the painting is considered stolen, and whoever has it has committed a crime, that person is not going to come forward very willingly."

Rodriguez shot her a deadly look. "Do you know where the painting is?" he asked.

"No, but it would be much easier to find it if the person who has it didn't have to face you and the police when that person returns it," Manuela said mildly. She looked very cool, but she was gripping her chopsticks so hard, her knuckles were white.

Rodriguez gazed thoughtfully at her.

One of his men came out of Manuela's office and said, "Hey, boss, we found it. Um, we found eight of it."

"Bring them out," he said. "Can these lights be turned up?" he asked, stepping back from the table without turning away from it.

Manuela rose and went to a bank of light switches near the door. She brought the lights up slowly so as not to scare anyone. The second floor gallery was now brilliantly lit. It was full of bright landscapes and still life oil and acrylic paintings from local artists. Even Rodriguez and his men glanced around the room before returning to the eight paintings lined up on a workbench. He turned each one over and shook his head. "Some of these have new canvas and new wood," he said.

"Some of the artists saved a little money painting over old work, Mr. Rodriguez," Manuela said helpfully.

"It must be unpleasant to be poor," Rodriguez said, looking into the middle distance. "I will take them all, just in case." He jerked his head at his men, and they started to gather them up.

"Those are all the copies, Mr. Rodriguez. Will the artists be left alone now?" Manuela asked his profile.

"Your artists are no concern of mine," Rodriguez said smoothly, turning away from her.

Manuela opened her mouth and closed is again. She took a steadying breath. "Will you convince Vogler to drop the theft complaint?" she asked.

"Vogler is a dog," Rodriguez said. "You ask him." He looked around the gallery once more and walked out.

At the sound of the front security door slamming, Manuela and Juan let their shoulders slump in dejection or relief or both.

Phalaxia stubbed Rodriguez's expensive cigarette out in the remains of her dinner and chuckled. "Who called Central Casting?" she asked, smirking at Juan and Manuela's shocked faces. "That's the most perfect villain I've seen since Ronald Reagan in 'The Killers.'"

Mornings in the Lee and Ross household were usually quiet. Including the answering machine, which was turned down low enough not to wake them too early. Like most LA musicians, Ross and Eddy screened their calls or they would never do anything but talk on the phone. If it was work or sex or something else as, or nearly as interesting they picked up; otherwise, they just listened and might or might not call back.

There was a flurry of calls reminding them both to come to Shorty's birthday that night at Eon, a new storefront club on Sixth Street around the corner from the Elks Club on MacArthur Park. Eddy and Ross smiled grimly at each other. Much as they liked Shorty, his parties tended to be too faggy for them. However, since the advent of Gregg Miller in the dancer's life, things around him had butched up. No telling what the party at Eon would be like; it was being held after the Lotus Room gig, which meant it would start at 2 AM. The guests would either be tired or wired and in either case, Eddy and Ross would put in an appearance and split early. Unless it was really swingin'; then no telling what they'd do. For Eddy, Hackenbush was a big factor in attending this party: if she was there and feeling friendly he'd stay until the cows came home.

There were a few work calls for Eddy and one about his teaching gig at the Guitar Institute of Technology. Eddy only taught when he had nothing better to do, and lately he'd been getting studio work and sending a sub to teach. GIT was wondering if and when they'd ever see him again. There were a few calls from women wondering the same thing. One of those women was Renee Soleil.

Ross, standing by listening for his own calls,

frowned violently enough to get Eddy's attention. "Hm, you're asking for trouble getting it on with that woman again," he said.

"I'm trying to retrace my steps to Hackenbush," Eddy said, jotting down a message about a gig. "Renee was the last woman before Mabel. Logically, Hackenbush should fall into my arms any day now."

Ross looked up from the message he was writing down and shook his head. "Edward, your sex life is a motherfucker."

"Ross, I have never fucked a mother that I'm aware of."

There were three hang-up calls that creeped them out a little. The caller didn't just hang up on the machine; it was like they were listening to the recording tape, like the caller could hear what was going on in the room.

"Who's calling you like that, Ed?" Ross asked.

"Why do you think it's for me?" Eddy asked back.

"Well, last time I broke up with a woman, she called like that," Ross said, looking him in the eye. "I knew it was her. I could just tell. I also know I haven't broken up with anyone lately–"

"You'd have to be fucking someone to break up with her," Eddy said, helpfully.

"–and you just broke up with Janet Tran," Ross finished his thought.

"Technically we didn't break up," Eddy said pedantically. "I'd have to see her to break up with her and she was never really with me because of that Emil guy. Y'know, her boyfriend."

"But it's her, isn't it?" Ross asked.

"I dunno," Eddy said, rubbing the calluses on his fingertips. "I'm too scared to pick up and find out."

"Why?"

"I don't want to be in the mess she's in," he said, shrugging. "If she took that fucking painting everyone wants, I don't want her fucking near me. And if she killed her boyfriend, that's really fucking scary."

"You sure can pick 'em, Ed," Ross said.

"Yeah, yeah, you'd think Hackenbush would rescue me from all these women, if she really cared."

"That's just it, Ed," Ross said. "She doesn't care."

Shorty Smith's twenty-first birthday party was an annual event in his circle and over the years had become an institution of sorts. However, when it fell on a work night, his older friends slightly despaired. Hackenbush at least admitted, very quietly and only to herself, that she was getting to the age where she just wanted to go home and put her feet up after a gig. Somewhere along the line she'd lost some of her enthusiasm for after-hours events, at least the ones that weren't paying her to sing.

It was possible that Shorty's party could have been held during the day, but that would have given some people an excuse not to attend. Although parties that started at 2 in the morning weren't for the faint of heart, they did remove any excuse of another engagement, work-related or not, for not attending. The party started at 2 AM; what else could anyone cool enough to know about it possibly be doing at that hour?

That year it was being held at Eon, a dimly neon-lit den of iniquity that probably didn't have a liquor license or even a business license, but as long as there was no trouble and exhausted emergency personnel could get a nourishing bowl of soup in the wee small hours from its motherly insomniac proprietor, no one ever said anything about the legalities of its existence. Eon might someday disappear like so many of its ilk, but until then, it was the place to be at quarter to three.

Which was exactly when Hackenbush strolled in. Her plan was to arrive when the party was in full swing, put in a dazzling appearance, dance with the birthday boy and be home by five-ish unless she was having fun, and then she might stick around a little longer. They did a pretty good breakfast at Eon for anyone with the stomach for heat-n-serve biscuits and dry scrambled eggs.

By the time Hackenbush got there the place was indeed swinging. There were two bands in action: Bruno Carlos and his Salsastra on one side of the room and a skiffle band on the other side. Miraculously, they were playing a shuffle grafted onto a tango; inexorably rhythmic, somewhat disturbing, and completely irresistible. Hackenbush screamed hello at the hatcheck girl (or boy, she couldn't quite tell), dumped her stuff in the relatively secure cloakroom and shoehorned herself onto the packed dance floor. It was more undulating than dancing, but it fit the unrestrained mood of the place as well. It was also too dark to see well enough to dance in there anyway. After saying hello by bumping against a few people, she retired to the bar and had a glass of grape juice because there wasn't any cranberry juice.

She leaned against the bar between Ross and Cody watching Renee Soleil dancing with Eddy Lee. "What the fuck is Renee doing at Shorty's party?" she asked, smiling viciously.

"It's a public place, isn't it?" Ross asked, and then stared her down.

She scowled and looked away. "She knew I'd be here," she said.

"I think she knew Eddy Lee'd be here," Cody said.

Hackenbush looked at her natty bass player. The handsome black man was the pulse of her band and, along with Shorty and Ross, one of the few men she could ever count on. Most of the time she found his wisecracks and jabs amusing, as long as they weren't aimed at her. This was not one of those times. "Yeah, right, well, it's a free country," she snarled. "Eddy can exercise his bad taste, bad judgment, and bad manners however he wants. It's nothing to me."

"Oh set it to music, Mabel!" Shorty was suddenly standing in front of her, hands on his hips, showing them how true bitchiness was done. "Have you seen Gregg?"

"Your Gregg?" she asked, stalling, hoping, praying Gregg Miller was about to walk in and save them all.

"Of course my Gregg!" Shorty yelled. "What other Gregg could possibly matter?"

Hackenbush glanced at Cody, who pantomimed drinking from a bottle. This only confirmed the blast of liquor-breath she'd gotten from Shorty's outburst. "Honey, have you been drinking?"

"Hell, yes, I'm smashed," Shorty admitted. "It's not easy being twenty-one all these years."

"Well, maybe next year you can be twenty-two," she said. "Just to break things up a little." She patted his angry cheek. "Me, I need some air." She nodded at Ross and Cody. On her way out she made sure to give Eddy and Renee a wide berth. They looked like they were fighting.

Not exactly fighting, but Renee wanted some answers and Eddy didn't want to discuss it. This was not unusual.

"Look, Eddy, is it me or Janet or God knows who else on your mind?" Renee was asking. She was furious and slightly drunk, too. "Or Hackenbush. I knew she'd be here tonight, the bitch."

"Don't call Mabel a bitch, Renee," Eddy growled. "It's Shorty's birthday, of course Mabel's here."

"Eddy–"

"Look, baby, not here and not now," he said. "My gig ends at nine on Monday, why doncha you come over then and we can discuss it, quiet-like, okay?"

She said something Eddy didn't catch as he was walking away from her. He'd seen Hackenbush heading for the patio and wanted a word with her.

Eon's patio was technically the alley with a few plastic chairs strewn about. At that hour nobody worried about vehicular traffic.  There was the occasional drunk or homeless person who wandered by, but the owner usually just gave them something to eat and they fell asleep behind the dumpster.

"Hey, Mabel."  Eddy offered her a cigarette.

"Ed."  She nodded graciously as she accepted the smoke and a light.  "I hear these might go to $2.25 a pack next year."

"That would suck very much," he said.

"Yeah, who can afford that?"  she asked, picking a shred of tobacco off her tongue.

"Wouldn't hurt us to quit, babe, we could use the money," he said.  "Um, Mabel–"

"Hey, have you seen Gregg Miller?" she asked suddenly.  "D'you know where he is?"

"Nope, I'm not keeping track of him," Eddy said. "Shorty upset?"

"What do you think?"

"Mabel–"

"Love!  It fucks you up!"

Eddy stared at her and then was distracted by the music.  The bands were playing a samba and a waltz at the same.  Hackenbush was listening, too.  "Wow."

"Dance?" he asked.  "I mean, we can pick one and switch if we don't like it."

She laughed and said he could pick it.  He picked the samba because he was more of a four-four man. Four-four was an honest, straightforward time signature. Three-four always made him a little nervous; it was sneaky, romantic and deceptively easy, and therefore easy to fuck up.  And then he felt stupid thinking that; meter is meter, just accept it.  Any other ideas on it were just the fucked-up romantic thinking of the breed of fools Hackenbush laughed at behind their backs because she couldn't even be bothered enough to hurt their feelings. At least that's what Eddy thought.

She was tough, all right, Eddy had seen that from

day one. It was only after he loved her and she loved him back that he saw the warmth and kindness and, well, love in the woman who could take care of herself and always had taken care of herself and always would take care of herself and might take care of a few people around her. Did she ever really need him? He wondered this for the nth time as he steered her over the asphalt. No, she never needed him, but she loved him and that had scared the hell out of him and he ran away from her. But he was back now; older, wiser; tougher and braver. Brave enough to pull her a closer and tilt his head toward her unsmiling lips.

"Back off, Ed."

"C'mon, Mabel," he whined. "It's just a kiss."

"There's no such thing as just a kiss with you, Romeo," she said, putting a handspan between them but never missing a beat in the samba.

To his credit, Eddy kept dancing, too. "Mabel, I love you, I can't feel this way about anyone else," he said.

"I have heard a version of this tune before, Ed," she said coolly. "And it didn't end well, as I recall."

"It's different now. I love you."

"Like you love Janet?"

"Now wait–"

"And Renee?"

"Mabel–"

"And God knows who else."

"I'm gonna kill Ross," Eddy growled.

"Don't threaten Ross," Hackenbush snapped. "Ross is too fine a person to notice the sordid details of your love-life, let alone tell me any of this,. My band is head and shoulders above this kind of gossipy bullshit. But the word gets around, Mr. Lee, and eventually–"

"It gets to you."

"I just hear it, baby, it doesn't get to me."

They stared at each other for a moment and then Eddy adjusted his grip and switched them to the waltz.

"You know, I'm not perfect, Mabel, but I was cooler when I was with you," he said, dancing in treble time. "I was faithful to you, you know that, don't you?"

"Edward, that was more than five years ago," she said. "What have you done for me lately?"

"Well, not as much as I'd like to do."

"Asshole." She almost smiled. "And you still can't waltz worth a damn."

Eddy saw this as weakening and pulled her close for a kiss. "Aw, c'mon baby. It will be like old times."

"Eddy, I said no."

"Try 'yes,' you'll like it."

"Ed, don't make me do this."

"Look, sugar–"

"Has that woman been bothering you about Janet Tran lately?" Hackenbush suddenly asked.

"Who?"

"You know, that crazy woman that's been bugging you? What's her name?"

"Ana Phalaxia?" Eddy asked, disconcerted by this shift in tactics.

"Oh, there you are, Mabel, as I was saying," Phalaxia emerged from the shadows of the dumpster, talking. "Oh, and Eddy, have you seen–?"

"It never fails," Hackenbush muttered.

"Jesus, Mabel, that was unkind," Eddy said, keeping Hackenbush between himself and the Phalaxia. "And possibly unnatural. Look, I don't usually gig on Sunday nights, can we talk then? Please?"

"I'll think about it."

"Around nine or after? Okay? Please?" he asked, backing away from Phalaxia and then dashing back into the club.

Hackenbush put her hand on Ana's arm. "Thanks for the rescue."

"I was wondering if you saw me," Ana said, dropping her weird sister act for a moment. "Glad to help. But he was saying some interesting things."

"I'd be much obliged if you'd forget them," Hackenbush said, suddenly very tired. "Or just keep them for your posthumous memoirs." Ana nodded graciously. "How about a ride home?" Hackenbush asked. She'd had enough of the evening. However, she did leave on an upbeat note: Gregg finally showed up and Shorty was very happy. Eddy caught her eye and gave her thumbs up, for which she suppressed a smile, but did sketch him a wave on the way out. Everyone else she knew there had either left or was too drunk to notice she was leaving.

The closest Hackenbush could park, and she was lucky, was two blocks away at Sixth and Coronado. Ana was quiet on the walk, partly because it was a dangerous neighborhood at that hour and they had to be vigilant, but mostly because she had a lot she wanted to say in the peace and privacy of the car.

They survived the walk to Hackenbush's Karmann Ghia, and she pointed it west on Wilshire as requested. "Where are you living these days?" Hackenbush asked.

"In a mystical commune in Koreatown," Ana said.

"Koreans?"

"Oh, heavens no," Ana said with a snort. "White people. Koreans don't have time for that bullshit. I'm just there because it's free and the food is macrobiotic. Far superior to the surfers I was with in Malibu. I do miss the sex though."

"Ah, too bad about the sex," Hackenbush said, downshifting to catch a red light so she could open a pack of cigarettes. "Did you really want to talk to me or were just rescuing me from Eddy?"

"Both," Ana said, accepting a cigarette and a light. "Although I do think Eddy's changed enough that you could get back together with him and no one would think less of you."

"Oh yeah? I'll bear that in mind." Hackenbush glanced around the deserted intersection and relaxed a little.  Two officers in a prowl car gave them a long look and kept going.  "How's he changed?"

"He's gotten smarter," Ana said, watching the cop taillights vanishing down Wilshire.  "At least smart enough to know you're the right woman for him for good."

"I think he's been working that out through a process of elimination, Ana."

"How unwise."

"But, maybe you're right," Hackenbush said, shifting into first on the green light.  "He's more together, musically, personally, financially these days.  I mean, we're all older..."

"True."

"Any Janet Tran sightings?" Hackenbush asked.

"She's not your competition."

"Oh, I know that," Hackenbush laughed.  "She ran off with that painting, didn't she?"

"That's what everyone thinks, Mabel," Ana said wearily.  "But the only thing we know is that she didn't kill Emil Vogler.  His father confessed to that."

Hackenbush slowed for another red light.  "Really? Why?"

"Well, it's all second- and third-hand, but what I've heard is that Vogler shot one of Rodriguez's men who broke in to look for the painting," Ana said.  "Rodriguez is a suspicious and thorough person, so he must have sent someone to toss Vogler's place just in case the painting was still there.  Stupid, but that's what we think happened–"

"Stupid and violent," Hackenbush added.

"Vogler shot this guy with the same gun that killed Emil," Ana went on.  "When the police took Vogler in for questioning, he fell apart.  He even admitted having Davido make the copy that he switched with the original so he could sell it to Rodriguez on the sly and collect the insurance money as if it were stolen–"

"Like he doesn't have enough money?"

"Who knows what enough money is for the Voglers

of the world?" Ana asked and went on. "Rodriguez and his lawyer talked to the police and Rodriguez admitted that he'd bought the painting, but he wasn't willing to report it stolen. So, if Janet does have it, she can return it to Rodriguez any time and we can all live happily ever after."

"Yeah, right."

"She's also off the hook for the murder rap," Ana said. "Although she could be in trouble for leaving the scene of the crime, if she witnessed the murder."

"How complicated," Hackenbush said. "But why did Vogler kill his own son?"

"I don't know, Manuela didn't know either."

"Manuela?"

"You remember, Manuela Alonso y Sierra? The new director of ELAG and the woman who introduced–"

"Oh, yes. I remember. How did she–?"

"Mr. Rodriguez has taken a liking to her," Ana said. "He drops by ELAG to chat now and then."

Ana directed Hackenbush off Wilshire and to a huge Craftsman style house south of Olympic. "I have two questions, Ana: is Rodriguez going to save ELAG for Ms. Sierra?" Hackenbush asked.

"No. And?"

"What do you think of 'The Threepenny Opera'?"

"It's brilliant. Why?"

"Just wondering. I'll watch 'til you get in the house." Most people in Hackenbush's experience used a door; Phalaxia climbed a trellis and vanished into a second floor window. On her way home, Hackenbush mulled over the performance artist's take on the new and improved Eddy Lee. Phalaxia was nutty, but she was often right. Hackenbush liked being right and prayed she herself would never get that nutty.

If Shorty was hung over the next day, it sure didn't show up in his dancing. Although he ate lightly at dinner and stuck to 7-Up all night, he tripped the light fantastic with as much joy and finesse as ever.

Hackenbush was more distracted. Not that an outsider could see, but enough to affect her timing, and get her scolded by Ross.

"Mabel, if you fall any farther behind the beat we're gonna leave you there," Ross said, adding a stern "Hmph" for emphasis.

"What? Are you double-parked, Ross?" she asked, the diva rising up in her. "It's a ballad, not a march. It can't be rushed; it must be nurtured, loved, fussed over–"

"Two bars on the word 'and,' Hackenbush, hm?" Ross asked. "This ain't an opera house or Birdland, woman, it's a... a..."

"Elegant lounge in a four-star hotel on the Pacific Rim?" Wang, the bartender, said helpfully. Then he even more helpfully poured them the drinks of their choice: vodka tonic for Ross and a Ramos Gin Fizz for Hackenbush.

"It's a bar, Hackenbush," Ross said, somewhat soothed by his well-made drink. "One where you sing standards fairly well, except when you get cute or lazy or stupid, so cut the bullshit and just sing, okay?" He smiled benevolently at her pout. "And now I must lecture Gregg on drinking too much before a gig."

"That poor kid cannot handle his liquor," Wang said, wiping the spotless bar.

"Wait, Ross," Hackenbush said. "Is... Eddy's usually home on Sunday nights, right? I mean, he said he was..."

Ross shook his head sadly. "He's usually around by ten, if he doesn't have a date," he said. "You comin' over?"

"I don't know," she said softly. "He's changed, hasn't he?"

"Yeah, but I don't know if it's for the better."

"What d'ya mean?"

"Eddy's traded stupid for ruthless, Mabel," Ross

told her. "He wants you back, but, well, he's not thinking if that's the best thing for you. Just what he wants, you dig?"

"Jesus, Ross, I thought you were his friend," Hackenbush said, shocked and pissed.

"I'm your friend, too, Mabel," Ross said. "And I remember how bad he hurt you once. And I don't want to see that again."

Had they not been standing in the elegant lounge in a four-star hotel on the Pacific Rim, Hackenbush would have hugged him. As it was she just laughed bitterly and said she wouldn't be over on Sunday.

"I thought something was starting with that scrawny artist guy... what's his name?" Ross asked.

"Arlo Mega. He's not scrawny."

"Yeah, him. Sparks flying?" Ross asked.

"Oh, kind of," she answered vaguely.

If nothing else, Hackenbush's extended conversation with Ross saved Gregg from a Ross-lecture, because it was time to start the second set. Shorty seemed to be doing a good job of nursing Gregg through his hangover, and the last thing they needed was Ross and Shorty getting into an argument over it.

The aforementioned Arlo Mega showed up in the middle of the set and sat at a table with a good view of Hackenbush. He ordered a Screwdriver and nibbled at the peanuts that came with the drink.

"Where've you been, Arlo?" Hackenbush asked on the break.

"Busy," he said. "My studio got tossed, it's not a pretty sight, and the police report took hours. It's all a waste of time." He looked and sounded miserable.

"Are you okay?" Hackenbush asked. She figured she could excuse his whining until she found out. "Were you there?" she asked. She'd heard at least one of the artists got knocked over the head when their studio was broken into.

"No, but it's a huge mess and I'm pissed off," he

snapped. "And where have you been?"

"Me?"

"Yes, you. I thought we were getting together, Mabel, and then you vanished."

"I didn't know we were on a schedule. Was I supposed to call you?" she asked with a nasty tone in her voice. Hackenbush did a lot of things, but chasing men was not one of them.

"That would have been nice."

"Then I'm not nice," she snapped. "And we're not getting together."

"Oh, c'mon Mabel," Arlo said sweetly, realizing how angry she was. "Why don't you come over after the gig and we'll talk about it."

"Come to your place?"

"Or I'll come to yours."

"At two in the morning?"

"Um..."

"Who 'talks' about anything at two AM, Arlo?" she asked nastily. "Most people just fuck at that hour."

"Um..."

She stood up and caught Wang's eye. "Wang, this gentl-, this person is leaving," she said, and looked down at Arlo. "Forget it, pal. That desperate, I'm not."

She flounced back to the stand where the band and Shorty were looking on with pinched little faces. They'd seen Hackenbush smack a number of guys down, but they liked Arlo and kind of felt sorry for him.

The only indication that Hackenbush was affected by any of this was that she was especially ruthless with the tempos, and glared at Gregg when he dawdled over a phrase she was through with. When Hackenbush was through with something, she moved on, and woe to anyone not hip to it.

When Sunday finally rolled around Hackenbush had several hours to mull over Eddy Lee's invitation to talk at his place. She was quietly grateful he'd invited her to his place because it was easier to walk out on him than throw him out if the conversation got bumpy.

*Dr. Hackenbush and her Orchestra* had Sundays and Mondays off from the Lotus Room gig and they kind of hated it. At least Hackenbush did; she'd rather be working than doing anything else, like thinking about money, sex, or politics.

But she was not working, she was thinking about Eddy Lee, who wanted to talk to her. She was also thinking about Arlo Mega, who'd called repeatedly to apologize for his boorish behavior in the bar and wanted to take her out, just to talk. She wasn't sure she had enough conversation for both of them; she knew she probably didn't have enough patience.

It would require strenuous measures to stop thinking about Eddy and Arlo, and to that end, Hackenbush got out a yellow legal pad and started scribbling notes on it. She made lists of names, places, events, costs, and contact numbers. After going through her address book and every scrap of paper in her purse, she broke down and called ELAG to get Phalaxia's number. She wanted to talk to Manuela first anyway, and she was lucky: Phalaxia happened to be there, mooching free food no doubt, at an Artist Talk.

"Glad I caught you, Ana," Hackenbush said when Phalaxia was on the line. "What?...No, I've never seen his paintings...They suck? Then I haven't wasted my time looking at them. What's that screaming in the background? He can hear you? Then maybe you should shut the fuck up about him...Oh? He's okay, but his work sucks. I still think you should shut up or close the door. Yes, I'll hold on."

She lit a cigarette while she waited for Phalaxia to get back on the line. "Yes, I'm still here...What did I want? Huh, what did I want? Oh yes! Manuela likes the idea, we found two Sundays next month—Yes, the month that starts in a week, yes, that month. Calm down, we all sight read and you've got total recall or whatever it is, we'll be fine. Look, I need you to call some people and ask them...Yes, they'll love hearing from you, got a pen and paper. I want to start with Renee Soleil. Yes, that Renee Soleil, there's only one I know of, isn't one enough of a burden?...Hey, you started it. Yeah, ask her, run it down for her: the where, the when, the how, and all like that. And don't tell her I said this, but Renee's a better sight reader than I am." Hackenbush smiled wickedly, knowing Phalaxia would tell this lie to Renee, and that would make the project irresistible to the bitch. She gave Phalaxia the names of two men to call and started to hang up. "What?... Janet? No, Ana, I haven't seen or even heard about Janet in days. Yeah, thanks, call me if anyone says no; I have more names. What? I'll call the cats on my list, don't worry. Bye."

Having killed a solid twenty minutes, Hackenbush went back to note making. Then she moved on to housekeeping, checkbook balancing, drank another cup of coffee, tried to get into reading "Cotton Comes to Harlem," but couldn't figure it out at all. Hackenbush tried very hard to be culturally sensitive, but anything set in New York City was beyond her ability to understand. And although she spent a lot of time with African-Americans, she'd never met anyone like the inhabitants of Chester Himes' Harlem, and rather hoped she never would. She wasn't overly fond of the police in the first place, so Detectives Johnson and Jones scared her some. But, she decided as she closed the book, it was more a geography problem than a race problem. Or perhaps it was just a literary problem; she found Himes' prose admirable, but more macho than she could enjoy just then.

"How annoying," she thought. "I'm back to thinking about men, damn them."

Of course the only cure for that was to sing for a while and then drag Anna Kodaly out for dinner. Anna was the sole proprietor of "Temporary Insanity," the best temp agency in Los Angeles for cash-strapped artists of all stripes. Insanity jobs had kept Hackenbush solvent more than once in the past. Anna ran her business, owned a house in Glendale, was loved and respected far and wide, and she'd done it all on her own with her business savvy, her people smarts, and her positive, but realistic outlook on life. She was one of the few people Hackenbush knew that she could talk to for hours and never talk about sex, clothes, or kids. It was just the kind of evening she needed. They went to Foxy's coffee shop in Glendale, the interior of which resembled a cross between a Swiss chalet and a pirate ship. They loved the place and had a delightful dinner, but even Anna noticed her friend was distracted.

"What's on your mind, Hackenbush," she asked over dessert.

Hackenbush sighed a little. "Eddy Lee."

"Who?"

"Oh, that's right you never met him. I guess you're not missing much. He's kind of a jerk. Or was. I was in love with him once."

Anna gave her immaculate blond hairdo a pat and lit a cigarette. "Oh, him. I didn't know you then, I only got to know you after he left," she said. "I can't imagine you in love."

"Neither can I," Hackenbush said, laughing good-naturedly. "But I seem to recall it was kind of nice."

"Nothing wrong with love, Hackenbush."

"That's how I feel about the ocean, Anna," she said. "They say you should never turn your back on it, and I don't, but I also don't like to swim too far from shore."

"How philosophical," Anna said, calculating the check split and tip. "I'll have to write that down when I get home."

"Don't forget to add eight percent to the tip for the waitress tax."

Because Anna kept normal business hours, it wasn't a late night. She was a sensible woman, so unless it was an emergency, it was never a late night with her. Hackenbush watched her drive off and sat in her car in the parking lot of Foxy's and had a long think.

Ross was enjoying a quiet evening at home all by himself when Renee Soleil showed up. "Eddy's not home," he said through the little latticed window in the door.

"He said he'd be home," Renee said. "Mind if I come in and wait? Remember how last time your neighbors freaked out because I sat on the steps all night and–"

Ross flung the door open. "Just come in, Renee," he said, and stomped off to read in his bedroom.

Renee knew her way around the kitchen of the house Eddy shared with Ross so she fixed herself a cup of tea and settled onto one of the two couches facing each other in the front room. She read through the Sunday Los Angeles Times, occasionally pausing to try to remember if Eddy had said Sunday night or Monday night. Well, she didn't want to be wrong and miss him, so she'd wait and ask him when he got home.

Instead of going directly home, Hackenbush drove to Rockaway Records in Silver Lake to flip through the dollar bin. It wasn't her night because there was nothing interesting enough to spend even a dollar on. She said hello to Tim, who was working behind the counter. "Slow tonight," she observed.

"We got a little of the Astro coffee shop post-dinner rush, but that was it," he said. "Sunday nights are pretty dead. We might get a few jazz fans when that new restaurant closes."

"Oh? Who's over there?" she asked, peering at the dimly lit café on the other side of Glendale Boulevard.

"Some guitar guy named Eddy Lee and his trio."

"It's a sign," she muttered. "From God."

"What?" Tim asked.

"I said, 'God, I wish they had a bigger sign over there. '"

"It's called the 'Swamp Lynx,'" Tim said. "No cover, bad food, and only beer and wine."

"Is zat so?"

"Zat is so."

"Don't fall asleep back there, Tim," she cautioned on her way out.

He grunted and went back to reading the Musicians Wanted ads in the Recycler.

The Swamp Lynx was practically empty when she got inside. She waved at Eddy, who, nicely supported by his bass and drummer, was doing interesting, possibly great things with "The Night Has a Thousand Eyes." After the last chord died away, he decided it was time for a break and came over to her table, where she was nursing a watery orange juice. "The joint's not exactly jumpin, is it?" she asked casually.

"Yeah, and dinner wasn't very good either," Eddy said. "And we'll see if we get paid, the owner split right before you got here."

"Think of it as an elaborate rehearsal," she suggested.

"Not a bad idea," he said. "You coming over tonight?'

She gazed thoughtfully at him and then shrugged. "Hey, why not?"

Eddy gazed thoughtfully at her and dug out his keys. "Ross should be home. Here's a key if he's not," he said, taking a key off the ring. "Still drink tequila?" he asked.

"Sometimes."

He handed her a twenty. "Would you get some for us?"

She said she would. "Want me to sing, Ed?" she

asked. "Might liven things up."

She sang "Some Other Spring" and "The Man I Love" to an empty room. Well, almost empty, the cook and waitress certainly dug it. She added "I Can't Get Started" as an encore and headed for the grocery store in high spirits.

About the time Hackenbush was on the second chorus of "I Can't Get Started," Ross was trying to figure out if he should let Janet Tran into the same house with Renee. "Eddy's not home," he said.

"Could I please wait for him?" she asked.

"Well, I guess," he said and stood aside. As far as Ross was concerned, the chips would have to fall wherever they did. He was just an innocent bystander in all this, whatever it was.

Ross could never figure out what Eddy saw in Janet: she wasn't especially beautiful, or musical, or interesting that Ross could see. She was short, kind of fat, and had such bland features, Ross had to remind himself who the hell she was every time he saw her. If she was spending money on Eddy, Ross had yet to see him with a nicer watch or a new guitar or a Maserati. But that was all Eddy's love-life, and Ross minded his own business.

"Oh, Renee..." Janet stopped halfway into the room.

"Janet! What the fuck? Are the cops still after you?" Renee asked.

"No."

"Then have a seat," Renee said, patting the cushion next to her.

"I was planning to," Janet said, heading for the couch opposite Renee. She wheeled on Ross, who was heading out of the room. "I brought Eddy a present. Can I put it on there?" she asked, pointing at the dusty mantle.

"I couldn't care less," Ross said, but he watched her unwrap a enlarged photograph mounted on a bulky background and set it on the mantle. "When the hell did that happen?" he asked, horrified.

"My God, Janet, what a terrible shot of Hackenbush," Renee said, taking a closer look. "Of course it's not your fault she looks like that. But Eddy and I look nice. You did a good job photographing that."

"I thought Eddy would want a souvenir of the evening," Janet said, settling on the couch. "I understand the three of you on one stage was a historic, never to be repeated event."

"You got that right," Ross murmured.

Hackenbush stood in the liquor aisle musing on tequilas. Not that there was a huge selection, but more than one is still a choice and cost and palatability had to be factored in as well. Then there was the other important issue: were they shooting or were they drinking like sane people? Shooting meant buying salt and lemons; sane drinking meant buying grapefruit juice and hoping Ed had some ice. Unable to decide, she bought two bottles of tequila (one for shooting and one for mixing), lemons, salt and grapefruit juice.

"There is no God," Ross said, staring at Hackenbush outside his door.

"Well, maybe so, maybe not," she said calmly. "But I'm not here to see God, Ross, I'm here to wait for Ed. Y'mind?"

"Ed's not here."

"I know, Ross, I just saw him at the club," she said, wondering what the fuck was up. "I mean, how unlucky: I show up and no God, no Ed. At least I know where Ed is. He's coming here. And soon. No estimates on God's ETA." She held up the key Eddy gave her to the lattice window. "And this is Ed's house key, he gave it to me, and I will use it if you don't open this fucking do–" Ross yanked the door open and stepped way back. Hackenbush stared, recovered like the trouper she was, and smiled, but only the lower half of her face got involved. "Oh... hel-lo, girls," she cooed at Janet and Renee. "Tequila anyone?"

Ross made a deep and mournful sound in his chest, but Renee sprang up and pranced into the kitchen like the spring lamb she wasn't. For a big woman, she could really move when inspired to do so. She was back in a flash with four tumblers.

"I'll need a shot glass and a knife, as well," Hackenbush said, hauling the bottles and fruit out of the bag.

Renee got four shot glasses, two serrated knives, and a cutting board.

"You really know your way around that kitchen, don't you, Renee," Hackenbush observed.

"We're just lucky Ross and Eddy are bon vivants who have a decent stash of glassware," Renee said. "Of course there isn't anything to cook with except a frying pan."

"What swingin' single man of the world needs more than a frying pan and a blender in the kitchen?" Hackenbush asked. She sat next to Janet and started quartering lemons. "Hi, Janet, what's new? You know the cops got Vogler for killing Emil?"

"I heard," Janet said, primly declining a shot glass.

Hackenbush looked at Ross, still by the door, standing there as if trying to decide whether to flee or not. "You drinking with us, Ross?" she asked.

He shrugged. "I guess. But I'm not shooting with you crazy broads," he said, and went into the kitchen. He came back with an ice bucket. "I'll mix mine over ice with that grapefruit juice."

"Ah, there's another thing every civilized man has in his kitchen: an ice bucket," Renee said.

"Don't be home without one," Ross said, pouring himself a mild tequila greyhound. Ever the gentleman, Ross asked Janet if she wanted one of what he was having.

She shook her head. Ross made her a drink and put it in front of her anyway.

"Are you okay, Janet?" Hackenbush asked

Janet nodded.

"Ana Phalaxia's been worried about you." Hackenbush poured shots for herself and Renee.

"Who's that?" Janet asked.

Hackenbush paused; she thought Janet and Phalaxia were friends or at least acquaintances. "She's a performance artist who's been worried about you." She licked the salt off her hand, saluted Renee (who was doing likewise), downed her shot, and bit into a lemon slice. She shuddered, and then smiled. "Been a while."

"Yeah," Renee said breathlessly, and then focused on Janet. "I think you know Phalaxia, Janet, she's the one who suggested Mabel and I sing together." She waved her hands at the photograph.

Hackenbush, who hadn't noticed it yet, sprang up for a better look. "Whoa, Janet! What a cool shot! You're really a good photographer."

Embarrassed, Janet looked at Ross, who merely smiled at her and sipped his drink. "I... Do you think so?" she asked.

"Oh, hell, yes," Hackenbush said, getting a closer look, trying to figure out what kind of thing the fabric the photo was stuck to was wrapped around. It was about the size of a small pizza box, but heavier. She gave up and flung herself back on the couch. "I mean, you must be great because Renee looks almost human in that shot."

"Oh, how amusing, Hackenbush," Renee trilled sarcastically. "I'm pouring."

"G'head. Lots more in these bottles," Hackenbush said, smiling pleasantly at everyone except Renee.

Ross sipped his drink, cursed Eddy Lee, and calculated his chances of survival if he had to break up a Hackenbush-Soleil catfight.  His rough estimate indicated that the odds were not in his favor.

"Well, lads, that wasn't completely a waste of time, was it?" Eddy was packing up after the gig.  They were as yet unpaid and somewhat grumpy.

"Was sure nice to play for Dr. Hackenbush again," the bass player said.  The drummer behind him nodded enthusiastically, adding, "Damn, that woman can sure sing."

"She has her moments," Eddy said cautiously, and they laughed at him.

The waitress came over, looking kind of nervous.  "Eddy?  There's a cop over there wants to talk to you," she said, nodding at a big guy in a shapeless coat sitting in the back of the café.  Eddy would have noticed him sooner or later; he was the only customer in the place.

Picking up his gear, Eddy headed for the back of the room.  "You wanted to talk to me, Officer...?"

"I'm Detective Mendez, Mr. Lee," he said, handing Eddy a card.  "I'd like to talk to you about Janet Tran for a moment."

Eddy groaned inwardly; he was really hoping the cops were going to leave him alone about Janet.  He had no fucking idea where she was and didn't even want to know.

Much to Ross's relief, two or three shots later the singers ran out of insults and switched to music.  Renee was doing a very good job with a song he disliked, "How High the Moon?," but Hackenbush was singing a cool and angular bass line under it.  Ross was inspired to sit in on brushes he made from the cellophane from a cigarette pack.

Renee swan dived into an abstract second chorus

and rode the razor's edge to a big finish. One false move, and the fragile web she'd spun from the song would have snapped in a nasty and painful fashion. It did not, and Ross raised an eyebrow in appreciation that she could do all that half-smashed on tequila. Most singers couldn't do that sitting on God's lap, if there was such a thing.

"Day-yam, Renee, I'm going to have to rethink that fuckin' tune," Hackenbush said, pouring shots. "There's more to it than I thought."

Renee accepted the compliment and the shot with equal grace. "Too bad you don't play bass, Hackenbush, you had some very cool ideas in there."

"I wrote a bass line like that for another song once," she said. "I wanted to use that descending half tone and perfect fourth riff to see how much I could fuck with the harmony and not mess up the song."

"What was the song?" Renee asked, pouring another round.

Hackenbush salted her left hand and said, "'You and the Night and the Music.'"

"Let's do that one next. Let's see what I can do to your bass line idea."

They toasted each other and downed their shots.

Ross found himself looking forward to more music. Then he looked at Janet, who looked at her watch and then looked pissed. "Hmmm," he thought. "The show must go on. Or something."

"Look, Detective Mendez," Eddy said. "I don't know where Janet is. I really don't know much about her."

"Why is that?" Mendez asked. "We understand you knew her pretty well."

"Well, yeah, we had a tawdry little affair, I guess." Eddy stammered a little. "I mean, I don't have much luck with women."

"How so?"

"Well, I don't treat them very well... they say."

"Who says?"

"Um, the women, some men friends I have, and, um..." Eddy was getting a little nervous. "Experts agree that I'm kind of a jerk to women, yeah."

"So you don't know anything about Janet Tran's disappearance?"

"She ran away, I thought... So, no, I don't."

Mendez gave him an unreadable look. "You wouldn't mind coming to the station and making a statement to that effect, would you, Mr. Lee?"

Eddy looked at his watch. "Could it be tomorrow?"

"Tonight is better."

"Can I make a phone call?"

"You're not under arrest, Mr. Lee," Mendez said. "There's no need to call anyone. Shall we go?"

Eddy had no choice but to follow him to the San Marino Police Station.

There was an odd fact about Hackenbush and tequila: after about five shots, she started to drink herself sober; numb, but sober. It was a cold, super aware sober, a kind of uber-sober, where every sense was hyped up and she was super mentally alert, if not paranoid, and yet detached at the same time. She also got really hungry after five shots, too. "I need pizza, Ross, where is there pizza?" Hackenbush asked. She was staring tragically into space for no particular reason. "Pizza that delivers. I can't drive."

"I can't stand up," Renee added, trying and failing to focus. "Janet?"

"I'm not hungry," Janet said tensely. "Shouldn't Eddy be home by now?"

"I don't know, Janet, I just don't know," Hackenbush said as Ross handed her a menu. "But I'll tell ya what I do know; that sunabitch is gonna pay for this pizza. We deserve this pizza after all this waiting."

"It all seems so unfair..." Renee began and stopped.

She closed her eyes and rubbed her temples.

"What does?" Janet asked.

"We're all sittin' here, waiting on Eddy, and why? Why are we doing this? Someone just tell me why." Renee asked.

"Oh why ask why, Renee?" Hackenbush said, studying the menu. "Because we're stupid? Who knows?"

"Yeah, stupid," Janet said and they all looked at her. "Yeah, stupid, stupid girls."

"Janet, what on earth were you doing with Eddy Lee?" Hackenbush asked.

"Fucking him," she said. "I wanted to do something crazy before I settled down with Emil. I thought Eddy was that thing."

"Poor Emil," Renee said.

"He was just as much of a bastard as his father," Janet said bitterly. "Emil said he wanted to do the right thing, but then it turned out he wanted half the Rodriguez money and half the insurance money. That's what they quarreled about. He even pulled a gun on his own father– and..."

"And?" Hackenbush asked.

Janet took a deep breath. "Emil was really drunk," she said. "We were upstairs in his room, with the painting, and he started to fight with his father. He keeps a gun in his nightstand and he drew it and aimed it at his father..."

"And?" Hackenbush asked.

Janet put her head in her hands. "His father took it away from him and shot him," she finally said. "I ran– I ran away..."

"And the painting?" Hackenbush asked.

Janet stared at her. "I–"

"Jesus, Janet. Have a drink," Renee said. "You need one." She poured the girl a shot.

"Thanks," Janet said, gulping her drink and looking away from Hackenbush. "I wish Ed was here. I came to break up with him, I want to get it over with." She grimaced at the rough liquor, but didn't stop Renee from pouring her another one. "I would have done it sooner, but..."

"Yeah, being on the run from the cops and the Mexican Mafia or whatever it is takes up a lot of time," Hackenbush said.

"It's a tough life for a woman sometimes," Renee said. "And men are pigs, present company excepted," she added waving to Ross.

"Renee, let's just get one thing straight," Ross said in his powerful baritone. "Men are not pigs; we're filthy pigs."

"And they let'cha down, don't they?" Hackenbush went on. "Take Janet here–"

"Oh, please do," Ross murmured.

"Emil gets shot, she's on the run, and where's Eddy?" Hackenbush asked, waving her arms around. "Where? Where? I ask you! Nowhere useful, the bastard."

"He's been here the whole time, Mabel," Ross said.

"And how useful is that?" she asked.

"Hm," Ross said, pouring himself and Janet another drink.

"He doesn't deserve any of us!" Renee yelled. "You, too, Ross, you're worth three or more Eddy Lees!"

"Thanks, Renee," Ross said. "I'm, ah, touched."

Hackenbush staggered over the phone and dialed. "But this is a woman's lot, isn't it? To wait, to wait, to wait, and wait some more." She turned to the phone. "Oh, hello there, Pizza Inferno, how long's the wait for an extra-large pizza with everything?...That long? Any chance you could pick up a bottle of tequila on the way?... No?...Hey, ya don't have to get nasty about it, pal; here's the address."

"And wait for what?" Janet suddenly asked and downed her drink. "Waiting, waiting, waiting! Is that all we can do?"

"Yes!" Renee cried, lurching forward. "And we're extra fucked that it's Eddy Lee we're waiting for!"

"Yes! Yes!" Janet said, starting to sound panicky.

"There's more to life than Eddy Lee." Hackenbush raised her voice. "We're all living lives that are less than they could be, and I'm going to do something about it!"

"Like what?" Janet asked, looking alarmed.

"I'm gonna get anchovies on this fucking pizza."

When Eddy finally got home he figured Hackenbush would have gotten fed up and split. Or she was a dream and waiting for him in his bed. He figured it was probably the first idea, but the second one gave him enough strength to find a parking space on his unusually crowded street and haul his gear up to the house. Hackenbush had his key, so he had to knock. Hopefully, she or Ross, if they were in there, would wake up and let him in so he wouldn't have to break into his own home. There were dim lights on in the front room; a hopeful and welcoming sign. He was very surprised when Janet Tran opened the door immediately. "Hey, Janet," he said, bringing his amp and guitar inside. "I was just talking to some policemen about you, and..." His eyes widened. "What the fuck are Hackenbush and Renee doing here?"

"They passed out," she said primly.

Eddy kind of doubted that Hackenbush passed out. She could hold her tequila; it did weird things to her head, but it didn't make her pass out. They were stretched out on their respective couches, neatly tucked-in with a pillow and modestly covered with a blanket. Eddy assumed that was Ross's doing; Janet didn't have that much maternal instinct. Renee had the toxic look of someone who'd passed out; Hackenbush just looked like she was sleeping heavily. But she was a weird drunk on tequila: she'd sleep, but only for four or five hours and then she was up, hung over, but functional. He twitched her blanket a little higher so her throat wouldn't get cold.

"The cops want to talk to you, Janet," Eddy said. He moved to Renee to make sure she still had a pulse. She did. "They say you're a witness to a murder that was in self-defense."

"It wasn't in self-defense, Ed," Janet said flatly.

"Tell the cops, not me."

She stared at him, her eyes overflowing with hate and hurt. "We're through, Eddy," she said, gathering up her coat and purse. "You make me sick. That's to remember me by." She pointed at the picture on the mantle. "Good-bye."

Eddy walked over to get a better look at the picture. "God damn, don't we look grand," he murmured. He didn't turn around when Janet opened the door, or when she stood there with the door open, or when she closed it softly behind her.

When he was sure she was gone, he cleared the pizza box, tequila bottles, lemon rinds, topped-up ashtrays, glasses, salt shakers, and remains of the Sunday LA Times off the coffee table. He made sure the front door was locked and fell into bed, asleep before his head hit the pillow. Whatever it was, he'd work it out in the morning, which was not far off.

Hackenbush woke up at the first grey glimmers in the room. Dawn in a strange place always woke her, hung over or not, and, looking at the unconscious Renee Soleil across the coffee table from her, she knew this was a very strange place indeed.

"Ah, tequila," she thought, carefully getting upright and hunting for her shoes. She ran backwards through the previous night's events—that was how it was with her and tequila: for better or for worse she had total recall, dammit—and eventually got to the photograph on the mantle and why it was there. "A parting gift for Eddy," Janet had said. Well, the photo was there, but no Janet; had she parted or was she...? Hackenbush vetoed looking in Eddy's bedroom; the way she was feeling, it could be nothing but trouble looking in there.

Getting carefully to her feet, she decided to wait for a drink of water until she got home. Orange juice wouldn't make her sick, but she wasn't about to see if Eddy had any in the kitchen. She wanted to split, but she also wanted the photo, which some small voice way far back in the back of her head said shouldn't take. "Fuck you, I'm taking it," she told herself, and very quietly took the photo and left.

One of the streets she usually took home from that part of town was blocked off with cops, so she took a big detour. Even though she was pretty sure she could at least drive home, the last thing she wanted was to try to pass a drunk driving test just then.

At home, she cleared her machine—yeses from all the cats she'd called the previous day—drank some orange juice, took a shower, a nap, and was nearly good as new by lunchtime. She ached a little and her skin was sensitive, but that was pretty mild hangover compared to other people's experience with the cactus.

After lunch, she spent some time looking at Janet's photo and the very bizarre way it was framed. She probed under the excess material at the back and found a letter taped to the coarse backing. "Ah ha," she thought. Unable to resist reading Janet's break-up letter to Eddy, she opened the envelope.

It was not what she thought it was going to be. It was not even close. She put it all in her closet, way in the back of her closet, and closed the door.

"That went very well! I feel confident that this will be an amazing, ground-breaking rendition of the 'Threepenny Opera,'" Phalaxia declaimed to the room at large because the musicians and singers were too busy packing up to pay much attention to her.

After a three-hour midday rehearsal in the

spacious and affordable Photography Center, the singers and the band had pretty much had enough of her anyway. Phalaxia was a brilliant choice as the narrator and various male parts for the ELAG fundraiser they were rehearsing for, but she was as much of a pain in the ass to work with as ever. Hackenbush and Renee, trading off to decide who'd sing Jenny Diver and who'd sing Polly Peachum, had spent most of the rehearsal one-upping each other, and had no time to manage Phalaxia. Everyone else thanked the music gods that Hackenbush got Lewis Lewis to conduct, which with this crew mainly meant directing traffic. It also meant keeping Phalaxia on track, cutting her useful but long-winded theorizing short, and keeping the other musicians from rising up and killing her. Luckily this was something Lewis, always an excellent pianist and even better music director (when he got the chance), excelled at.

Personalities aside, it had been a tough rehearsal. Except for Phalaxia, who had total recall or something, they were all highly trained, well-disciplined professional musicians who could sight read and follow a conductor at the same time. They'd all had their scores and tapes for a week, which meant they were individually prepared, but would be hard-pressed to work as a group. Even with Hackenbush's savage pruning and clever arrangements to get it to a little over an hour, it was still a lot of music and singing to get through. The two express run-throughs, with a break for snacks, were tough on all of them. On the first run-through, Hackenbush sang Jenny Diver; on the second, Renee sang her and stole all of Hackenbush's best ideas. That was okay because Hackenbush stole all Renee's licks on Polly Peachum. The guy singing Macheath was too cool to let on how impressed he was by this. The rest of the group was too intimidated to mention Hackenbush's and Renee's singing, but, as a consequence of their covert awe, they played up to the level of those performances. Phalaxia expressed neither awe nor fear; she was above it all and, as narrator and singing Mrs. Peachum and Lucy Brown parts here and there, had enough to do. However, she did step in to settle the dispute over who sang the "Pirate Jenny" song, which could be either sung by Polly or Jenny depending on the production, and gave it to Jenny thus making the song ratio a little more even for the chick singers.

"Well, we lived," Hackenbush said quietly to Renee.

"I salute you, Mabel," Renee said equally softly. "You really had Polly and Jenny swingin' today. I'm sure Herr Brecht was spinning in his grave." She nodded at Hackenbush's polite laugh. "Phalaxia was stiff as a board. Does that worry you?"

"Not really," Hackenbush said. "I gave her a tape of the Lotte Lenya recording of the whole show and Bobby Darin's version of 'Mac the Knife.' Knowing Phalaxia, she'll puree them together somehow and at the very least..."

"Yeah?"

"...It will be interesting." Hackenbush smiled at Renee's snort. "Phalaxia's the backbone of this thing. She was just trying to get it right today."

"I heard my name," Phalaxia said into Hackenbush's ear.

Hackenbush recoiled. "Jesus, Ana! You're gonna kill me someday."

"And how long have you been standing there, Ms. Phalaxia?" Renee asked.

"Long enough to agree with Hackenbush," Phalaxia said. "It's such a rare occurrence, I almost enjoyed it. This will be a good show; too bad we're only doing four performances."

"Nobody can get away for more than that," Eddy said. He and Ross were on the gig and had a few questions. "Mabel, I've been hearing rumors all week that cats can sit in on this gig. Is that right?"

"WHAT?" Lewis yelled from across the room. He had great ears; all music directors have great ears.

"Sure, why not?" Hackenbush said. "I mean, all we've got now is a rhythm section."

Lewis also had great legs and he used them to cross the room in three leaps. "Are you mad, woman?" he yelled. "This is enough of a zoo as it is."

"Think of it as a challenge, Lewis," Renee said, coming to Hackenbush's defense because she herself was guilty of inviting cats to sit in as well. "They can just, y'know, play along with the singers. Everyone knows the show a little, more or less; those horns won't get in the way."

"Of course they won't get in the way, Lewis," Hackenbush cooed at him. "You can conduct a jam session; I've seen you do it!"

"When?" Lewis asked.

"Um... Maybe it was more of a vision," Hackenbush backpedaled.

Lewis fixed everyone with his icy blue glare and squared his shoulders. "No more invites," he said in his best music director voice. "We have enough problems," he added, staring at Phalaxia before he turned smartly on his Florsheim heel and stalked out.

"See ya Sunday, Lewis," Hackenbush called after him. "At ELAG."

"What a bad tempered man," Phalaxia said. "Am I a problem?"

"No, just an unknown element," Hackenbush said.

"Feh." Phalaxia almost pouted as she put her script and libretto in the plastic bag she used as a briefcase. "Oh, by the way, Janet Tran's funeral is tomorrow." She looked at the four shocked faces around her. "I guess you didn't know."

"When did she die?" Ross finally asked.

"A week ago Monday," Phalaxia said. "It was a

gang shooting, a drive-by or drive-along-side, as well as I can figure from the LA Times. Lots of bodies, Latinos and Vietnamese; seems it took the police a while to figure out it was her."

"Where?" Hackenbush asked, hollowly.

"Somewhere over by Wilton and Beverly," Phalaxia said, waving at one of the guy singers. "Well excuse me, my ride home is getting antsy. Are you going to Pam Tucker's art opening tonight? No? A shame."

"Christ, I drove by it on the way home," Hackenbush said after Phalaxia was gone. "There were cops everywhere."

"How long before the cops figure out how close that is to your house, Eddy?" Renee rather sensibly asked.

"I dunno," he said.

"Maybe we should go to the police," Ross suggested. "Tell them she was with us–"

"I don't think so, Ross," Eddy cut him off. "They were looking for Janet as a witness to Emil Vogler's murder. Well, they found her. Case closed."

"That's pretty cold, Ed," Ross said.

"Ross, how many people are dead over this?" Eddy asked. "Aren't you sick of it? Or you, Mabel? Or you, Renee? I'm sorry I ever heard of Janet Tran or any of this fucking mess."

They all nodded and picked up their stuff. Their time was up and the Photography Center caretaker was giving them dirty looks because judging by the girls in bikinis, what looked like a swim-suit shoot was trying to set up around them.

"Hm, yeah, our house getting tossed the other night wasn't so great either," Ross said on the way out to the parking lot.

"When did that happen?" Hackenbush asked.

"The night after you all were there," he said. "They didn't take anything, or break much, just pulled everything out and went through all the cabinets and closets."

"Huh," Renee said. "Same thing happened at my place a few days ago."

"Did you call the police?" Hackenbush asked. They shook their heads. "Why not?"

"Nothing was taken or damaged," Renee said, getting into her car. "And I don't like talking to policemen, Mabel, do you?"

Ross and Eddy just shrugged. Ross said he'd see Hackenbush at the gig later on and split. "Wanna go to Langers for dinner, Mabel?" Eddy asked.

"If it wasn't a gig night, I would," she said. "Are you okay, Eddy?"

"Yeah, maybe, I'm bugged about Janet," he said. "She was so mad at me that night, last time I saw her, I kind of feel bad."

Hackenbush put her arms around him. "I'm sorry, Ed. She was mad at everyone that night." Eddy hugged her back. "Look, I don't have time to talk right now. Are you working tonight?"

"Nope."

She sighed. "So... why don't you fall by the Lotus Room and pick up the keys to my place?" she asked and got a wicked smile in return. "We can talk when I get home."

"Just talk?"

"I get home around 2 AM," she said. "We can talk, too. I'll see you later, okay?"

"Okay." And there probably wasn't a happier man than Eddy Lee in all of Los Angeles at that moment.

Arlo Mega, on the other hand, was not a happy man. It was bad enough he wasn't getting anywhere with Hackenbush, but to have to run into Ana Phalaxia at Pam's opening and listen to her go on and on about the show she was doing with Hackenbush was just too much for him.

Hackenbush had been ignoring Arlo's calls and letters and the few times he'd actually gone to her place, she'd never shown up. Well, never shown up in an hour at least, which was all the time he had to wait on her front steps. Her neighbors were the watchful type, too, and even though no one spoke to him, he knew he was being watched and that would unnerve any man.

He did know she was at the Lotus Room that night and roughly what time she'd be home. This would be his last-ditch effort, his all or nothing, the make or break, or at the very least the night when he would figure out if she was worth all the stress or not. She probably wasn't worth it—no woman was—but Arlo styled himself hopeless romantic, and sometimes he had to live up to it. He drank a little more standard-issue art opening cheap white wine and once again wondered if there wasn't some kind of cheap white wine tanker truck that stopped at all the galleries in Los Angeles because it all looked and tasted the same at every opening Arlo had ever been to, and he'd been to a lot of them.

Around midnight, as they were getting ready for the last set and after Eddy Lee had picked up the keys to Hackenbush's place, Ross narrowed his eyes at the singer and said, "I hope to God you know what you're doing, Mabel."

"With Eddy?" she asked. "Sure I do, Ross. He's still Eddy, isn't he?"

"Like you're still Mabel?" Ross asked, and got frowned at. "People don't always change for the best."

"I know, Ross," she said. "But I have to find out for myself." She smiled wryly at him. "And if it blows up in my face again, I'll know how to handle it better."

"What blows up in your face?" Cody asked from behind his bass.

"Love! Cody! Love!" she cried, raising her hands to heaven. "What else blows up in a woman's face?"

"The transmission on her car?" Gregg suggested, plugging his guitar amp in.

"Pressure cookers?" Shorty asked, standing like a stork to stretch the tops of his thighs.

Hackenbush exchanged shrugs with Ross. "I don't know what's worse, working with cynics or comedians."

When Eddy got to Casa Hackenbush, he was a little surprised to find a guy sitting on her front steps. "Uh, could I help ya, pal?" he said, trying to sound tough and reasonable at the same time.

"No."

"Well, ya can't stay here," Eddy said. "This is my girlfriend's house and–"

"Your girlfriend!  She's my girlfriend," Arlo shouted. "Or she should be." He stared at Eddy's shocked face for a moment. "Hey, I know you, you're that guitar player, Eddy, um..."

"Eddy Lee, that's me." Eddy looked a little closer. "Hey, aren't you Arlo, that artist guy."

"Yep."

They shook hands and then shrugged manfully. "So, what are you doing here?" Eddy asked.

"Waiting for her.  You?"

"She sent me over here," Eddy said, shifting the grocery bag of booze so he could get out Hackenbush's house key. "See?  I have her key."

"And I have a mission," Arlo said loftily.

"And I have a gun so open the door and get inside."

They had not seen the tall dark man with the soft voice come up behind them, but they did what he told them to do.

There were actually two of them, well-dressed Latinos with good skin and sleek guns.  One of them kept his gun on the guys while the other made a sweep of Hackenbush's vintage one-bedroom plus dining room non-rent controlled house.  After that, he stepped onto the west-facing veranda and signaled someone because two more dapper Latin-types with guns came in with an older man, who was even better dressed and conspicuously unarmed.

"How awkward," the older man said pleasantly. "I was hoping to wait for Miss Hackenbush alone. But perhaps that's what you both are here to do as well."

Eddy shifted his grocery bag uneasily. "What do you want with Mabel?" he asked.

"She has something that belongs to me," the man said. "A painting."

"Oh God," Arlo said softly. "Are you Mr. Rodriguez?"

"I am indeed," Rodriguez said urbanely. "It is interesting to find you both here, Mr. Mega and Mr. Lee, but not unpleasant. I have been most impressed with your painting, Mr. Mega, and very much enjoyed your performance at Vogler's party, Mr. Lee. Especially during Miss Hackenbush and Miss Soleil's duet." He turned to one of his associates and asked him to turn on some lights.

Hackenbush had two illumination settings: bright and dark. The place flooded with light, showing off either her eclectic taste in home furnishing or the mishegoss of cast-off stuff she lived in, depending one's point of view. Whatever it was, it was tidy: the piano was dusted and polished, the battered hardwood floor was swept, and the worn-out couch and armchair only had a few books and papers on them.

Rodriguez invited them to have a seat on the couch. "What's in the bag, Mr. Lee?" he asked. One of his men took the bag and showed him. "Ah, tequila. Not my favorite brand, but it would be pleasant to have some now." He strolled around the house, looking at the books and pictures, turning on lights, while one of his men went into the kitchen for glasses and ice. He settled into the armchair and poured three shots over ice.

"Thanks," Eddy said, accepting an old-fashioned

glass of his own liquor. "Why do you think she has the painting?"

"Because you don't have it and Miss Soleil doesn't have it," Rodriguez said.

"I thought Janet Tran had it," Arlo said, grimacing a little. It was good tequila, he just wasn't used to it over the rocks.

Rodriguez smiled coldly. "It was not found with her body."

"Well, good luck tonight," Shorty said after the last set.

"Thanks, darlin'," Hackenbush said, snapping her ukulele case shut.

"I think you're doing the right thing," he added.

"I sure hope so."

"I mean, I don't like Eddy," Shorty said thoughtfully. "But, hey, I'm not planning to fuck him. Well, night!"

Hackenbush watched him and Gregg walk out. Through luck or karma or fate, they'd made themselves a happy home and Hackenbush was happy for them. Even when she was slightly pissed off at Shorty, like just then, she was happy for him. She looked over her shoulder at Ross and Cody.

"Mr. and Mr. Gregg Miller seem to be having a good night," Cody said.

Hackenbush laughed. "Yeah, well, we know Shorty can dance, but Gregg's turning into a killer guitar player."

"Better than Eddy Lee?" Ross asked.

"Eddy Lee who?" she said, and left on his laugh.

If Hackenbush had a credo, it was always leave 'em laughing.

"To Mabel Hackenbush!" Rodriguez raised his glass. "An extraordinary woman."

Arlo and Eddy chimed in with his toast.

"Yeah, she's swell," Eddy said. "I don't think she's got your picture, though."

"Really? Why?" Rodriguez asked.

"She's a sensible woman," Eddy said lightly. "If she had it, she'd've handed it over to the cops by now."

"I agree with that," Arlo said, clinking the ice in his drink. "Mabel doesn't like complicated stuff. She likes it simple."

"But her singing is very ornate," Rodriguez said, pouring another round. "I was very impressed by her performance that night, at the party."

Eddy nodded. "She was showing off for Renee," he said. "The fancy stuff was fine, but the counterpoint she was singing under 'Body and Soul' was built a fourth above the root chord structure, with little syncopated mordents and legato trills, which gave it that crazy, almost Gregorian chant-like feel. That chick can hear things sometimes that just blows my mind." He looked intensely from Arlo's and Rodriguez's puzzled expressions. "It's almost like she's making an arrangement for a larger group, an orchestra even—you know she can orchestrate, don't you, Arlo?" he suddenly asked.

"I didn't know that."

"Well, she can," Eddy said, nodding enthusiastically at Rodriguez. "So when she's singing what she's hearing in her head, sometimes it only makes sense to her, 'cuz she can hear the string section and we can't."

"But there was no string section at Vogler's party," Rodriguez said.

"Exactly!" Eddy took a swig of his drink to punctuate his point.

Arlo and Rodriguez stared at him, and then Arlo shrugged, and said, "Musicians are crazy."

"Crazier than artists?" Rodriguez asked. "I've been visiting ELAG. I've had some odd conversations there. Although not as odd as this one."

"When I finish a painting," Arlo said after a sigh.

"I can hold it in my hands, give it away, destroy it. It exists. When Hackenbush and Eddy finish a song, what do they have? Nothing."

"Not nothing, Arlo," Eddy jumped in. "We have, um, a memory, a feeling, maybe a recording."

"Yes, a shame that performance could not be recorded," Rodriguez said. "Or have some kind of memento of it. Like a photograph."

"Ah," Eddy said, and stared hard into his glass. "A shame."

"At least you got to hear it, Mr. Rodriguez," Arlo said. "I was stuck in the drawing room with all the fake paintings and Miss Cuban Lady freaking out."

"You mean Miss Sierra?" Rodriguez asked with some menace. "Do not insult her."

"I– Sorry, I didn't mean to," Arlo mumbled.

"I understand." Rodriguez stood to stretch his legs. "Miss Sierra is an intense woman in a difficult position. She is an outsider trying to fix problems she doesn't understand. Her organization's problems are Chicano problems, and yet she runs to a white man, Vogler, for help. And he betrays her."

"But the Chicanos ran it into the ground," Arlo said. "And then they wouldn't help her raise money."

"Because she has no power," Rodriguez said. "And they don't fear her."

"She just wants to make ELAG a place where everyone can make art again," Arlo said. "What's wrong with that?"

"Art is useless," Rodriguez said loftily.

"Then why are you so hot to find your painting?" Eddy asked.

Rodriguez stopped pacing and fixed him with a cold eye. "Because it has power now," he said. "I promised it as a gift to a man I respect. That painting has my honor on it now."

"That painting's got a lot of blood on it now,"

Eddy said. "Emil, that painter guy, Janet, and for what?"

"Ask Vogler," Rodriguez said. "He tried to cheat me, his insurance company, ELAG, the Mexican consulate, Janet." He chuckled. "What a fool. So unnecessarily complicated."

"Complicated," Arlo said thoughtfully. "Davido was the painter guy's name, Eddy. I studied with him. He was uncomplicated; he just wanted to paint. Then he got complicated because he wanted money for his paintings, and no one wanted to buy them. Any idea what happened to him, Mr. Rodriguez? I won't tell anyone, I just want to know for myself."

Rodriguez raised his eyebrows. "I believe the police report said he startled an intruder who shot him," he said. "The only thing worse than startling an intruder is arguing with one and not answering questions. Or so I am told." He sent one of his thugs into the kitchen for more ice and poured another round. "A foolish old man, no power, not even any honor left in him. Very sad, very bitter."

"And very dead," Arlo said with some heat.

"We will all be dead someday, Mr. Mega," Rodriguez said philosophically. "It is how we live now that matters."

"Exactly!" Eddy said, cutting off whatever Arlo was about to say. "And that we keep living so we can do it right. Or something."

"Exactly, Mr. Lee, exactly," Rodriguez said distractedly. They all pricked up their ears at the sound of a car parking outside.

Seeing her house ablaze with lights lifted Hackenbush's spirits so much she did a little dance when she got out of her car and completely failed to see the local gang kid waiting for her.

"People in your place, Señora," he said from the shadows of the tree in her neighbor's yard.

"God, you scared me," she said, peering into the gloom, but not going any closer. "Shouldn't you be over at Eastlake Park?" she asked.

"Men in your place," he repeated.

"I'm expecting someone," she said.

"More than one."

They both jumped a little at the voice from the window behind the tree. Hackenbush's neighbors were fresh-off-the-boat Chinese, so they always surprised her when they spoke English. Only the men and boys ever spoke to her and very seldom at that; the women just smiled and nodded. "Too many cars," the male voice continued.

Hackenbush looked at her street and spotted Arlo's truck parked a little ways from Eddy's van. "Oh, dammit," she hissed. "Two men."

"Too many men," the voice in the window said.

The Eastlake boy agreed. "Too many men and too many cars," he said.

Hackenbush didn't understand that last bit; she only saw those two cars. She shrugged and figured she better face the music. The sooner she tossed Arlo out, the better for everyone.

"Señora..." the Eastlake boy called after her.

"Thanks, kid, I got it covered," she said, heading up her stairs and into her house.

She walked in and found Eddy and Arlo on the couch facing her. "Look, guys–" And then the arm around her throat and hard metal object jammed into her side gave her something new to think about. "Please don't kill me," she said.

"I hope not, Miss Hackenbush, I'm looking forward to your performance at ELAG next Sunday." Rodriguez stepped into the room and smiled calmly at her. "Where's the painting?"

"The painting?" Hackenbush winced as the gun, she assumed it was a gun, poked her harder.

"Mr. Lee and Mr. Mega have been having fascinating conversations while we were waiting for you, dear lady," Rodriguez said, coming closer. "They both make a living with their hands. Whose fingers shall my associate start breaking? Mr. Lee's perhaps?" He nodded and a thug grabbed Eddy's left hand.

"Uh, Mabel!?" Eddy squeaked out.

"Don't hurt him! Don't hurt him, please! I'll tell you!" Mabel yelled as loud as the arm around her throat would let her.

Rodriguez held up a hand and his thug let go of Eddy. "Where?" he asked.

"It's..."

"Yes?" Rodriguez moved closer.

"It's in the trunk of my car."

"Your keys, please?" he asked politely.

She handed them to him; she could see her car from where she stood. "Tell your guy the trunk is in the front, not the rear," she said. A few seconds later, Rodriguez's employee waved the canvas at them and walked off.

"I'm glad you understand how simple it is, Miss Hackenbush," Rodriguez said, straightening his cuffs. "Too bad everyone isn't as intelligent as you are," he added on his way out.

The musicians and painter stayed very still until they heard Rodriguez's cars drive off. "Um, Mabel? Do you still have my painting?" Arlo asked.

"The copy of the Siqueiros canvas?"

"Yeah."

"No, Arlo, I just gave it to that guy," she said, pacing a little.

"Oh, my God." Eddy buried his face in his unbroken hands. "So how long before he comes back and kills us?"

"Could be a while," Arlo said thoughtfully. "I tried to make my canvas really look like the Siqueiros.

I aged the wood, scuffed up the sides, painted over an old canvas, and yellowed the backside of it. I wanted it to be more than a copy, more like an art-thing than just a reproduction." He paused to down his drink. "So he'll be back in the morning, instead of later tonight, unless he gets a look at it in really good light or takes it to an all-night art appraiser."

"Who was that anyway?" Hackenbush asked, holding the nearly empty tequila bottle up to the light and then pouring what was left into her mouth.

"Tomas Rodriguez, who else?" Eddy asked.

"Huh," she said, flopping into her armchair. The three paused to listen to sirens in the distance, but there are often sirens in Lincoln Heights at that hour. "Should we call the cops?" she asked.

"And tell them what?" Eddy asked. "That we gave a fake painting to a killer? They'd laugh us into next week." He picked up the empty tequila bottle. "Got more booze, Mabel?"

"Just gin."

"We should not switch to gin," he said sadly. "Seriously, Arlo, how good's your fake picture?"

"Not good enough to fool an expert, and an amateur would figure it out eventually," Arlo said. "What should we do?"

"The best we can," Eddy said blearily.

"Well, first you two should sober up," Hackenbush said. "Then we'll figure this mess out. But, you know, I wasn't expecting you both tonight and you're too drunk to toss out." She didn't want to admit it, but she was more rattled than she seemed and didn't want to be alone just then. "What should we do now?"

Arlo and Eddy exchanged speculative looks.

"Let me rephrase that," Hackenbush said firmly. "What should we do that doesn't involve sex in any way, shape or form?"

They wound up drinking orange juice and playing

rummy until dawn. Shortly after she won the first game, Hackenbush realized she didn't have her car keys and went outside to look for them. In her neighborhood, she half expected her car to be gone, but she hadn't heard it being driven off, and, lo and behold, there were her keys in the driver's side door. She closed and locked the trunk. As she passed her Chinese neighbors' mailbox, she made a point to look at the name written on it. Street light in the wee small hours isn't the best to read by, but she made out that it was 'Nguyen,' so maybe they weren't so Chinese after all.

Dawn made them feel soberer, if not safer. As they sobered up, they began to realize that they'd have to tell the police their lives were in danger and, being men, talked Hackenbush into doing the dirty work. "Why me?" she asked.

"Well, they came to your house," Eddy said, gathering up glasses and escaping into the kitchen to wash them.

"And we were just here by accident," Arlo added, going into the kitchen to help Ed.

This was a strategic error on the lads' part because she followed them in. "All right," she sighed. "But I insist on getting some sleep first, so dry your hands and get out."

Hackenbush managed to sleep and procrastinate until it was time to get ready for her gig at the Lotus Room. While warming up, she hit upon the brilliant idea that she'd fall by Hollenbeck Station on her way home. It would be nice and quiet at that hour and she could tell her story to the guy at the desk and be done with it. She had no idea if they could do anything to protect her or Eddy or Arlo, but she figured she should at least give them a chance.

And, by God, next time her neighbors told her there were men in her house, she'd call the cops immediately. On her way to her car, the curtain in her

Asian neighbors' window fluttered. It was the same window the guy had tried to warn her from. Both neighbors, Asian and Latino, had tried to warn her. Why hadn't they been clearer? Was it a language problem or were they just naturally cagey in Los Angeles? Ah, goddamned multiculturalism again: my culture doesn't warn you clearly enough so your culture can get killed so my culture can have your house. Or something. Of course she had had Eddy Lee on her mind last night and so was not thinking clearly and probably missed the warning. Yeah, it was all Eddy's fault; that made more sense. On the other hand, if her multicultural neighbors would just call the cops– "Oh, don't be silly, Mabel," she told herself. "Even you don't call the cops in this neighborhood." Hackenbush had never had any problems with the Hollenbeck cops, they all seemed like cheerful guys. But she was white and wasn't especially afraid of the police. Even so, she steered clear of any trouble that might involve the police and when she did have to call them, such as when a fight broke out under her windows, she always called the desk and made them promise not to send an officer to her door. The Hollenbeck cops understood: they sent a squad car to the area, but never sent a uniform to her place.

Once she got to the club and had a nice dinner, she began to feel safer. Cody asked her how it went with Eddy.

"Oh, fine," she said. "Except Arlo was there, too, and that crazy man who wanted Janet's picture was there with guys with guns and I gave him Arlo's copy of the picture, and I have to go explain all this to the cops later tonight because he's going to kill us all when he figures out he's got a fake picture."

They all just stared at her. "That's what Eddy said this afternoon," Ross said. "He also said you're going to the cops."

"I will after the gig," she said, stuffing a tempura yam into her mouth.

"But what happened with Eddy?" Shorty finally asked.

"Ah. We were a little stressed out, Shorty, so we just played cards until the sun came up and then he and Arlo went their separate ways," she said.

"Eddy also said that," Ross said.

"See? Confirmed by Ross," Hackenbush said sharply. Ross just smiled at her.

"I think your romance with Eddy might be jinxed," Gregg, happily-living-with-Shorty, said.

"Gregg! Please! We shouldn't give up on them," Shorty, already-convinced-the-Hackenbush-Lee-romance-was-doomed, said.

"Married people will never understand," Hackenbush said to Ross, who was the only other unmarried person at the table. "I think I'm jinxed with all men. I probably could have worked it out with Arlo, he only really slipped up once, and for a self-absorbed painter, that's not so bad." She looked at her watch and folded her napkin. "Of course if Rodriguez is going to kill us all, it's probably moot. Shall we, cats?" She led the way to the bandstand and picked up her baritone ukulele. She asked Wang, the bartender what he wanted to hear: he said "Moonglow," so "Moonglow" it was. The moment the first note left her mouth, her troubles—man and criminal—were far away.

Towards the end of the second set, a large lady came in and Hackenbush thought she looked familiar. Hackenbush was too polite to stare, but she was wracking her brains as to where she's seen her before. "Piper's coffee shop? Nah? Lorthen-Perez Gallery? Nah? Wait, she's an art maven. That's right, Miss Cuban Lady. Friend of Phalaxia! Oh no! Wait, maybe she won't appear if I just think her name. Yeah, heh heh heh." This pathetic theory went to hell about five minutes later when Ana

Phalaxia joined Manuela Alonso y Sierra at their tiny cocktail table. If Phalaxia and Sierra could be combined and equally divided, it would have been enough table for them both, but as that was impossible, they were pressed for space. At least Sierra had the good sense not to try to fit her generous ass onto a bar stool.

Hackenbush hated having Phalaxia in her audience. Phalaxia sneered at any actually enjoyable music, preferring the atonal compositions of Webern, and Berg (especially the opera "Lulu"); the dissonance of Charles Ives, and the unspeakable serial and chance music horrors of Hackenbush's contemporary and fellow Grove School graduate, Sukie St. Athanaus. Having not only survived, but understood, Sukie's last concert, Hackenbush put up a shrine to Cole Porter for a few days.

Nevertheless, Hackenbush felt obliged to saunter over to their table on the break. "Hullo, ladies, what brings you to this den of iniquity?" she asked.

"We came to tell you Tomas Rodriguez is dead," Phalaxia, never one to stand on ceremony, said. "He died in your neighborhood. Know anything about it?"

Hackenbush stared at her, "What?"

"Mr. Rodriguez is dead," Sierra told her. "There was a shooting on the freeway. His car and another car both crashed and everyone was killed. It was very early this morning."

"Which freeway?" Hackenbush asked, stalling, trying to figure out how much she should tell them.

"The 5 Freeway," Phalaxia said. "Just north of the Broadway exit."

"Well, yes, that is Lincoln Heights," Hackenbush agreed. "If you can really count the freeway, I mean, the freeway really belongs to the city at large, more than just the community, and–"

"Mabel."

"Ana, I don't know a thing about Rodriguez

getting killed," Hackenbush said, having finally arrived at the section of the truth she could deal with. "Lots of people die on the 5 Freeway, why ask me about it?"

"Do you remember Juan Aguilar from the meeting at ELAG a few weeks ago?" Phalaxia asked.

"Sort of," Hackenbush said, wondering what Phalaxia was on about. "He's a community guy, gang counselor guy–"

"He's a youth counselor." Sierra nearly snapped at her. "He's been very helpful to ELAG in communicating with the Latino and Vietnamese communities–"

"Yeah, too bad their gangs hate each other guts," Hackenbush said. "Oh, I know, I know. I lived in Santa Ana when the Boat People first showed up. Those Vietnamese boys kicked some Latino and Black ass. Has that changed any, Ms. Sierra?"

Manuela looked into her empty glass. This made Hackenbush feel slightly bad, so she waved at Wang for another round. "You can put these on my tab, Wang," she said. "So what the fuck is up, girls? My break's almost over."

"According to Juan, the other car was full of Vietnamese men," Phalaxia said. "Boys really–"

"Gang members, really?"

"Yes. When Janet was killed, the other car was full of Latino men, young men," Phalaxia continued. "What Juan thinks is that one of Rodriguez's second or third string groups looking for the painting followed Janet and killed her. But the painting wasn't with her. Then Juan heard that Janet had been at a house before the shooting and they were trying to find out who was there with her. They were keeping an eye on the house, and were looking for who arrived after Janet and who left the next morning. According to Juan, all they had on those two other women were the makes and license plates of their cars." Phalaxia took a sip of her drink. "Now, I know Eddy's place was searched, and Renee had her place searched. I called Renee before we came here, but she wouldn't tell me who else was at the house with Janet that night. Was it you?"

Lucky for Hackenbush there was a commotion by the door and she got up to rescue Arlo from Wang. "I think we can lift the ban on this guy, Wang," she said.

"Anything you say, Hackenbush," Wang said pleasantly. "What'll you have, sir?"

Arlo ordered a Tequila Sunrise. "I got a very crazy call from Pam Tucker," he said. "She says Rodriguez is dead."

"Really?" she asked after a moment. Arlo nodded. "Then I'm very glad to see you, Arlo, old man," Hackenbush said, comradely clapping him on the back. "I have to get back to work, but you now have the delightful job of telling Phalaxia and Miss Cuban Lady all about last night with Rodriguez. Don't leave anything out, or Phalaxia will use thumb-screws on you." She scribbled on a cocktail napkin and shoved it at the artist. "Oh, and here's Ed's number. Would ya mind calling him later so he doesn't lose any more sleep? Thanks, Arlo, you're a real pal!"

For the next set, Hackenbush had a very entertaining view of Phalaxia's sneer and Sierra's shocked face as Arlo told them about the previous night at her place. Was it so worthy of contempt and shock? She wondered, but couldn't be bothered to worry too much because she was so relived she wouldn't have to go to the police after the gig.

Arlo split before the end of the set, but Phalaxia and Sierra hung on so Hackenbush strolled over to answer Ana's question. "Yes, I was there that night with Janet," she said. "But there's nothing to it, Ana, except one thing."

"What?" Ana asked. She was putting on her coat and sounded as if she couldn't care less about the answer.

"Janet was okay," Hackenbush said. "I think

she was trying to do the right thing by protecting the painting from the Voglers and Rodriguez. She just didn't realize she was in over her head." The three women nodded. "So, I'll see you Sunday for the show at ELAG," Hackenbush said. "Maybe we can dedicate it to Janet."

"Maybe," Phalaxia said, sounding very tired.

"Oh, by the way, what was the name of the guy from the Mexican counsel that was at that meeting at ELAG last month?" Hackenbush asked.

"Mr. Acuna, Juan Acuna," Sierra said. "Why?"

"I was getting him confused with Juan Aguilar." Hackenbush went back for the last set. Phalaxia and Sierra were gone next time she looked.

Gone, but not forgotten, because Wang misunderstood her and instead of two drinks, put the whole table's entire bill on Hackenbush's tab. "Goddam multiculturalism," Hackenbush thought, signing off on the bill. "I can't even communicate with Wang anymore.

Incredibly, the story got even stranger by Sunday. Juan Aguilar was a one-man rumor mill that afternoon before the fund-raiser performance at ELAG. Hackenbush was too keyed up in pre-performance nerves to listen with more than half an ear, so she wasn't sure if Mr. Vogler committed suicide in custody that week or the week before. She overheard Juan saying, "The police say it was suicide, but the word is that hanged himself with someone else's belt."

"Can you only commit jailhouse suicide with your own belt?" Hackenbush asked Phalaxia, who shushed her.

"And Enrique Morales was gunned down in Quito. No one knows over what, but probably a drug cartel thing," Juan was saying.

"Who?" Renee asked, saving Hackenbush the trouble.

"You know, the lawyer Rodriguez bought the

painting for," Phalaxia said.

"You're so much better at keeping track of this stuff than I am, Ana," Hackenbush said. "You really ought to give up performance art and start solving mysteries. I know I'd like you to do that in, say, somewhere glamorous, like San Francisco or New York. Yes, mysteries or family therapy; I'm sure you'd excel at either." She turned away from Phalaxia's scowl so she could laugh quietly at her own joke.

"So, the guy in Bolivia–" Eddy began.

"No, Ecuador," Juan corrected him.

"Yeah, wherever, that Rodriguez bought the painting for is dead, so there's no one looking for the painting anymore?" he asked.

"That's what we're all hoping," Juan said. "Most of Rodriguez's former associates thought he was crazy to go after it like he did."

"Crazy or egotistical?" Hackenbush asked. She winked at Renee. "You know there's nothing quite like the male ego when it gets all revved up."

"Yes, yes, no telling what a man will do when he thinks his dick's on the line," Renee observed.

"Oh, the horror," Phalaxia chimed in.

Their conductor and music wrangler, Lewis Lewis, cleared his throat and said, "That's really interesting, girls, but we've got a show to do. Let's go, everyone."

Musicians and audience very dutifully took their places. Manuela offered a brief introduction and thanks for the cast's fund raising effort on behalf of ELAG, even though it was too late to save it. She hoped the last month of ELAG's existence would be as beautiful as its heyday. She, herself, would be very sad to leave the beautiful city of Los Angeles and return to her home in New York.

"Then why the fuck are we doing this?" Renee whispered at Hackenbush. She was slightly annoyed because Hackenbush won the coin toss and would be singing Jenny that night.

"Because we're nice, ELAG still needs money, and we like Kurt Weil's music very much," she whispered back.

Lewis conducted the truncated overture and cued Ana in her first song, "Mack the Knife." Hackenbush said a little prayer because Ana, who was not primarily a singer, got off to a rocky start, but started to swing after a few bars. The singers added finger snaps and the occasional "hup, hup!" and Phalaxia was off like a swingin' rocket. The rest of the show went extremely well, with a few bumps due to lack of rehearsal, but they all sang and played with tremendous soul and passion. Hackenbush scared the hell out of everyone with her version of "Pirate Jenny," Renee was a wicked Polly Peachum, Ana's narrations and songs kept the show moving along, and the guys singing Macheath and Mr. Peachum were almost as menacing as the late Mr. Rodriguez, though not as well-dressed or well-spoken. And the finale absolutely brought the house down; although Manuela seemed a little upset with Hackenbush afterwards, everyone else thought it was a fantastic show.

Hackenbush was too busy eating and drinking and receiving accolades to pay much attention to either Arlo or Eddy. Arlo got a minute in the buffet line to congratulate her. "Too bad you can't do the whole show," he said. "You were great up there. Terrifying as Jenny, really."

"Thanks, darlin', but it's such a long show," she said. "I chopped out all the parts I thought were boring so we could do it oratorio style."

"I really liked the part where all the singers stepped in front of the music stands for the finale," Arlo said. "I thought you were going to kill us all."

"Ah, then we succeeded," she said, giving him a sisterly pat on the shoulder before she was dragged off to chat with a philanthropist/art-collector-interested-in-multiculturalism who'd admired her mono-cultural-Western-European performance. He mentioned a recent Broadway production called the "3 Penny Opera" with Sting that Hackenbush was unaware of. "How timely, how interesting," was all she said before she could escape to the bar and a glass of industrial-strength, standard-issue art gallery white wine.

Eddy finally got her alone as she was leaving. "I've been meaning to ask you, did you take Janet's photo?"

"I did."

"Why?"

"I wanted it," she said. "Did you want it back?"

He said he did, and she said she'd bring it by later in the week. Maybe they could have lunch one day.

On her way home, she stopped by Rocky's Pizza around the corner from her house and bought a small mushroom pizza and an empty small pizza box.

"Thank you for seeing me on such short notice, Mr. Acuna," Hackenbush said, when they were in his office and the door was closed.

"I'm happy to make time to see you, Dr. Hackenbush," he said, urbanely and in lightly accented English. "I enjoyed your performance last night very much."

"You know, I enjoyed it, too."

"I was wondering, though, what kind of doctor are you?" he asked.

"No kind, that's just a nickname from when I was a kid and wanted to be a veterinarian like Hugo Z. Hackenbush in 'Day at the Races' that's all," she said. He said, "Ah," and she figured that was her cue to get down to it. She held up Janet's strangely mounted photograph. "This letter is for you," she said, drawing the envelope from the back of the frame. "Janet really wanted your museum to have this painting," she said while he was reading. "I like that bit in the letter about how a nation's art belongs to the nation that produced it. I'm not so sure about that, but I'm happier for your museum to have this picture than for guys like Vogler and Rodriguez to have it."

"I see Mr. Vogler Sr. signed this," Acuna said, thoughtfully. "When Janet and I spoke to him, he was adamantly against donating the–"

"Have you ever seen Vogler's signature?" Hackenbush asked. Acuna shook his head. "Me, neither, so let's just assume that's Mr. Vogler's signature. Or maybe he signed it just to get Janet off his back, figuring he was going to scam the insurance company and Rodriguez, so it didn't matter what he signed. I doubt anyone left alive cares anymore. Except you and me. And as soon as I leave, I don't plan to care anymore either. I think if we take the muslin off this frame, your painting is under here." She handed it to him and he carefully removed the thumbtacks inside the wooden bars and then the muslin the photograph was glued to. Janet couldn't have done a better job disguising or protecting the Siqueiros canvas. Hackenbush silently bowed down to her.

Acuna stared at the painting that had caused so much trouble, so much death. "Of course we would like to thank you for returning the–"

"Actually, Mr. Acuna, I think you should just quietly take it to Mexico and leave me out of it," she said, gathering up the photo-mounted-on-muslin. "Bad things seem to happen to anyone around that picture. Maybe it's luckier in Mexico. Where Janet thought it belonged."

He nodded and put the painting in the closet next to his desk. "There was something I wanted to ask you last night, but Ms. Sierra seemed to be having a very angry conversation with you then," he said, offering her a coffee, which she declined. "I'm not an expert on 'The Threepenny Opera,' but I believe you changed the words in the finale. I don't recall them being 'First comes the food stamps, then comes the multiculturalism.'"

"Yeah, Manuela was a little upset about that," Hackenbush admitted. "But I think she was more upset that ELAG is closing at the end of the month. So if you want to buy some Chicano art at bargain prices, you better get over there soon."

"I see."

Hackenbush turned to go, and then turned back. "You know, Mr. Acuna, I'd like multiculturalism better if it was part of the struggle for universal healthcare and better jobs. Add justice in there, and I'm your girl. But all I see multiculturalism doing is making us fight over stupid stuff—like whose art is cooler—when we should be fighting together for a better world, or even just a better Los Angeles. I mean, you can't eat multiculturalism, so it's only for people who already have everything else."

"'First comes the food stamps?'" Acuna asked.

"Then comes the shelter and healthcare and job and education for everyone willing to play by the rules and work for it," Hackenbush said. "Then we can argue over why I should love Ranchero music and Los Four more than I do."

"I wish you luck, Dr. Hackenbush," Acuna said, giving her a microscopic bow.

"Thanks, Mr. Acuna, but I'm not the one who needs it."

On the way to Eddy Lee's place, she wrapped the muslin-mounted photo around the small pizza box, which it fit perfectly. "Well," she told herself. "He just wanted the photo as a memento, right?"

Several months later Phalaxia forwarded a photocopy of a news clipping she claimed was from Manuela Alonso y Sierra, now residing in New York City. The blurb was in Spanish, but Phalaxia scrawled a translation under it, which read:

"'Siqueiros painting, a generous gift from the Vogler family and Ms. Janet Tran, has been installed in the National Art Museum in Mexico City.'"

And under that was scrawled:

"Manuela said the Vogler heirs put up a fight, but since no one could prove the signature on the donation letter was a fake, the Siqueiros is permanently home in Mexico. I don't suppose you know anything about this, do you, Mabel? No? I thought not. I remain yours in the arts, truth, justice, and, yes, my dear Hackenbush, in multiculturalism as well. Ana Phalaxia."

Hackenbush laughed a little and went back to playing her baritone ukulele. She had the Lotus Room gig that night and the show must go on.

Other books by Ginger Mayerson

Dr. Hackenbush Gets a Job

Dr. Hackenbush Gains Perspective

Electricland

The Pajama Boy

Darkness at Sunset and Vine

www.ingramcontent.com/pod-product-compliance
Lightning Source LLC
Chambersburg PA
CBHW070501130626
46555CB00003B/1106